PARABLES OF
SARAH BLACKSTONE

Jason Mayer

Happy Duck Publishing
111 East 3rd Street
Belle, MO 65013

Genre: Fiction, General
ISBN: 978-1-7369596-5-7
First Edition.

This book is dedicated to my mother. I miss you a little every day. And some days I miss you even more.

CONTENTS

PROLOGUE

"I'll say it again… man is the cruelest animal."

– Fredrick Nietzsche

The Cage

The young girl moaned as she sat up. A loud crash on the wooden floor above her had pulled her from a welcomed slumber. She strained to hear what had made the noise; horrified that it was likely one of the monsters that had visited her during the many weeks she had been held prisoner in her cage.

She began to shiver. She wasn't certain if it was from fear or the cold seeping through the hard, concrete floor. The sheer silk wedding dress she had been forced to put on provided no warmth in the dank basement.

Her stomach growled with hunger, but that was the least of her pains. Her wrists were sore from the countless times she had tried to free herself from the handcuffs. Her ankles were even worse. She could feel that the cold shackles holding her damaged feet together were slick with blood.

Her eyes were covered by a pair of swimming goggles that had been blackened by shoe polish. She had tried to pull them from her face, but the strap was cinched too tightly on her head. Her mouth was covered by an elaborate leather gag that was wrapped around the back of her head and laced together with tight stands of paracord.

She began to cry. She didn't want to cry, but the tears came anyway. She knew crying would just spur on the monsters. They reveled in her fear and her pain.

Another loud banging noise caused her to start. She knew it wouldn't be long before the monsters descended the stairs. In her panic, she lashed out with her legs and hands. She knew it was futile, but she needed to do something.

She pushed past the agony in her ankles and pulled hard, trying to free one of her feet. The effort was no different than the hundreds of other attempts she had made. She laid her head back on the floor and pulled her arms over her head.

As she stretched out her hands, she could feel bits of trash all around her. She had done this before, finding nothing but fast food wrappers and other bits of trash. She reached out further this time, pushing past the pain.

That is when she felt it; something new, something hard and cold. Possibly metal. She understood that

she would have to stretch farther than she had ever
done before if there was any hope of reaching the
item.

She pulled against the shackles with all her
strength. The pain was excruciating, but she no longer
cared. She felt a pop in her foot and she pushed back
another couple of inches. She was not free from the
shackles, but something had dislocated between her
ankle and foot. She screamed out in pain as she laid
back and reached out for the object.

She felt around carefully until her finger tips
glided past a hard, slim handle. She clawed at the
handle until the item scooted close enough for her to
wrap her fingers around it.

She pulled herself into a fetal ball and gripped the
item with both hands. She inspected it and quickly
discovered that it was a small, folded up pocket knife.
Working quickly, she managed to open the knife and
expose the blade.

Her mind began racing. What should she do with
her newfound weapon? Maybe she could defend
herself from the monsters. But that was foolish. She
was only a child, and there were at least three
monsters. She might be able to wound one with the
small knife, but that would only enrage the others.

Maybe she could cut off her goggles and gag. But,
even then, she would never be able to get out of her
metal restraints; especially not with them lurking
above her right now. She was surprised that they had
not descended the stairs as soon as they had heard
her cry out.

Panic set in as she realized she did not have much time to decide on a course of action. She was desperate to be free of her prison. But her options were slim.

She closed her eyes and tried to focus, and then a cold reality overcame her. In her clarity, she realized there was only one way she was going to get free of her prison and stop the monsters from terrorizing her.

She began to cry again. Her lips trembled as she repeated the Lord's Prayer. She couldn't remember all the words, but she hoped he would understand.

She gripped the small knife as tightly as her battered little fingers could and raised her arms high. She wasn't sure where to aim, but figured the center was the best option.

She squeezed her eyes shut and slammed the knife down as hard as she could, plunging the sharp blade into the middle of her stomach.

TRADING MOONSHINE
FOR BEAVERS

"Tragedy is like strong acid. It dissolves away all but the gold of truth."

– D.H. Lawrence

Spring 2004

A Glass of History

Sarah Blackstone-Fosterman cut the wax ring and uncorked the bottle. She poured herself a glass of the fifty-year-old rye whiskey and sat the bottle on the table, spinning it so that she could see the label. She looked at the maker's mark, which was a faded black image of the original Blackstone family crest.

She sniffed the cork to confirm the liquor was still good. The smell of the peppery rye brought back memories of working with her dad at his backwoods still as a young girl.

She sipped the smooth whiskey and closed her eyes, letting the memories wash over her. She hadn't had a drink of hard liquor in a few years, but she really needed the memory of her father to comfort her tonight.

Her family was broken, and there was nothing she could do to repair the damage. Katie, her precious ten year old granddaughter had been kidnapped, brutalized, and murdered by an evil man named Jim Powers. And now she had to find a way to keep her sons from killing the man and bringing even more pain to the family.

Just a few months ago Katie had gone missing while riding her pink bike around her small subdivision. Katie's mother, Lisa, began to worry when she missed her check in time, and started looking for her. That worry turned into panic as the minutes turned into an hour.

Soon the police were called. Then the FBI arrived to lead the search when Katie's bike was found in a neighborhood field with spots of blood on the handlebars.

Everyone in town pitched in to help look for the child. Eventually, her body was found in an old barn past the edge of town. The investigation started with interrogations of everyone in the family. The men in the family were quickly ruled out because they had been working in the family furniture store showroom, which had cameras. Lisa had to endure hours of questions only a day after finding out her daughter had died.

The speculation about Lisa did not end until the lab reports showed that Katie's killer was male. However, the reports also showed that their precious Katie had been raped. This news was earthshattering for everyone.

The small-town police were not accustomed to dealing with such a high-profile case. They brought in more than a dozen suspects," eager to make an arrest to calm the community.

The lead detectives worked quickly to build a case, too quickly in most instances. They questioned people even after they asked for lawyers. They tried to coerce confessions. They even took DNA samples without warrants or legitimate cause.

Jim Powers was one of the men brought in with the

original group of potential suspects. As the investigation proceeded, signs started to point to him. The evidence was overwhelming: The barn belonged to his uncle. His DNA was found on Katie. Throughout the short investigation, other evidence began to mount against the man. It should have been a slam-dunk case. But shoddy policework made getting a conviction nearly impossible. It was determined that the DNA was collected illegally, which negated the strongest physical evidence.

A video tape of the interview with the suspect revealed that he had asked for a lawyer before the detectives started asking questions. His entire interview was deemed inadmissible. Plus, the evidence collected at the barn was also thrown out because the location of many key pieces were discovered during the interview.

The district attorney decided not to move forward with pressing charges until new evidence could be found. Without the DNA reports, interview tapes, and evidence gathered at the barn, it would be nearly impossible to make a case. He told the Fostermans that he needed more time to build a winning strategy.

The district attorney promised to keep the case open as long as it took to gather more proof, but everyone knew it was hopeless.

Katie's father, Mark, was outraged by the news. He spoke frequently about ways to make the known killer pay. Lisa slipped into a deep depression, locking herself in her room and not accepting food.

Sarah's youngest son, Paul, was her major concern.

He had taken the death of his niece extremely hard, and he was beyond outraged. As a former Marine, like his father, he was a man of action. He was no doubt planning to do something very violent, very soon.

Sarah's husband, Lucas, tried his best to calm his two sons, but his sadness was overwhelming. When the boys looked at their broken father, it made them want to lash out at Jim Powers that much more.

Sarah had called a family meeting earlier that afternoon and did her best to calm everyone. She pleaded for them to give law enforcement and the DA more time to make their case. She knew there was little hope of the tides turning in the court at this point, and even less hope that the family's anger and sadness would subside anytime soon.

Everyone had promised to let things play out for another two weeks before they met again as a family to decide what to do next. That meant she had two weeks to figure something out.

Sarah took another swallow of the whiskey and let the liquid warm her insides. She was trying to channel her past life in the backwoods of Kentucky. What would her father do in this situation?

When Sarah was very young, her father had been a moonshiner. He had plenty of experience skirting the law and dealing with unsavory characters. She had seen him navigate several precarious situations, and she was hoping one of those memories would shake loose a way out of this situation.

After the third sip, she remembered an incident her

father called "trading moonshine for beavers." He liked to give silly names to his stories, and she remembered hearing him tell the story while sitting around the still one night when she was about nine years old.

In the liquor business it was considered against the honor code to snitch on anyone regarding their booze making operations. No matter how much of a competitor or what the situation may be, divulging where a still or stash of liquor was hidden was always an unforgivable sin.

If this code was ever broken, the shiner who committed the offense would be blackballed throughout the area. He would never be able to buy supplies, sell his bottles, or do business in the region ever again. And this was only the beginning of the punishments that could be handed out.

At one point, her father had come across a particularly vile competitor named Tipton who had been caught contaminating a working batch at one of her dad's hidden stills. Her father chased him off by putting bullet holes in his truck, but the competitor continued to cause trouble by stealing his customers and trying to cut off his supply chains. Her father was forced into action, but he had to honor the code.

Her father knew that Tipton made money through other illegal means, including hunting beaver pelts, which was a federal offense. Her father stalked the man for a few days and discovered that he was skinning and storing his pelts in an old barn on some land at the edge of a federal reserve. He delivered an anonymous tip to the U.S. Game and Wildlife agency, and two federal wildlife officers were sent out to investigate.

When the officers arrived, they found Tipton climbing over a fence that divided federal land from the private farm. A shootout ensued and Tipton was eventually taken into custody and sentenced to fifteen years in prison.

The memory of the story made Sarah smile as she recalled how bombastic her father could be after a few glasses of whiskey.

She knew that Jim Powers had a couple prior felony offenses, and if he was sentenced for any new major offense he would face a long prison sentence. That wouldn't provide justice for Katie, but it might just buy the time needed for her family to heal.

Now, she just needed to find a beaver pelt to pin on the vile man.

Stalking Her Prey

Lucas was an early riser, and he always left the house for the showroom by eight and stayed there until early afternoon. This gave Sarah plenty of private time to conduct her investigations into Jim Powers.

For the past three days she had been leaving the house just a few minutes after Lucas and driving over to Jim's auto repair shop. She had watched as various customers entered his shop, hoping to catch him in some illicit act.

She had seen nothing out of the ordinary, just people bringing in their vehicles to get inspections or to fix one problem or another. She was frustrated that she hadn't seen any obvious signs of wrongdoing. For some reason she expected it to be easy to find him doing something illegal.

It was nearly noon when she saw a pretty blonde haired woman pull up in an older model Ford Taurus. She got out wearing jeans and a Led Zeppelin t-shirt. Sarah immediately recognized her as Jim's wife, Janice. She walked up to the open garage bay where Jim came out to meet her.

He grabbed a bag of fast food from her hands and opened the top. He rooted through the bag before looking up and asking a question with a scowl on his face. Janice said something that angered him, and he raised his hand like he was going to slap her. He stopped short when she flinched away from him.

More angry words were exchanged before she turned back towards her car. Sarah was able to get a better look at her face from the new angle and saw a dark shadow under her left eye.

That was the break Sarah needed. She had seen enough domestic bullies in the backwoods of Kentucky to recognize a wife beater when she saw one. Janice's flinch was enough evidence to let her know that the event happened on a regular basis, and the fading black eye meant that he probably hadn't gotten his power fix in a couple days.

She waited until Janice pulled out and circled around behind her. She had an idea of where Jim

Powers lived, but wasn't sure of the exact address. The Ford Taurus circled through the Wendy's drive-through window before heading back to the shop. Janice delivered the corrected order to a still angry Jim before getting back on the road.

Sarah followed her out of town until she turned onto a gravel driveway about a mile outside of the city limits. Sarah didn't make the turn, but instead continued driving slowly on the highway where she could still see the Taurus.

She pulled over on the side of the road and watched as the car pulled up in front of an old farmhouse. It was a small box of a house with a tin roof, faded wood, wide front porch, and uncovered windows.

She had a good line of sight to the house from the side of the highway, but she was fairly exposed in her current location. She drove down the road a bit and found an access road that was mostly grown over with weeds. She popped her Jeep Wrangler into four-wheel high and followed the bumpy road up to a cattle gate.

From this new location she was even closer to the house. Looking around, she couldn't see any cars from the highway, which meant they probably couldn't see her. This location would work, but she would need some better equipment to conduct a proper stakeout.

Red Handed

Sarah arrived at home at four in the afternoon and pulled her white Jeep up to her workshop at the back of the house. She went into the workshop and opened her safe.

The safe held a collection of her guns; including her Accurate Ordnance precision competition rifle, a couple of nice shotguns, and a few other assorted long guns that she had inherited from her father. On the door were five different pistols, including her Glock 17 9mm pistol. She grabbed the Glock and put it in a leather paddle holster.

She grabbed her shooting bag from the bottom of the safe and slipped the Glock inside along with a box of shells. She opened one of the side pockets to find her hearing protection earmuffs which also had an amplification feature. She changed out the batteries in the earmuffs just to be safe and stuffed them back in the pocket. Next, she grabbed her pair of high-powered Swarovski binoculars and strapped the large piece of equipment across the top of the bag.

That should be everything she needed for the mission, other than her cell phone of course. After loading everything into her Wrangler, she went into the house where she found Lucas working on dinner. He was halfway through preparing chicken parmigiana, which he knew was her favorite.

She poured them both a glass of red wine and sat down at a stool at the kitchen island to keep him company. They spent the evening eating together, before Lucas left for his weekly poker game with his friends at around eight o'clock. She knew he wouldn't be back until at least midnight, which should give her plenty of time for her impromptu stakeout.

She grabbed her cell phone off the charger and jumped into her Jeep. It was a bit overcast now, and the clouds were blocking out the light of the moon. By the time she arrived at the farm road, it was pitch black out. She turned off her headlights and only used the parking lights to find her way to the gate.

Once there, she pulled out her binoculars and ear protection. She looked through the large binoculars and could see into the front windows of the small house. There were two windows, one that looked in on the living room and the other into the kitchen. She could see Janice sitting on the couch reading a magazine. She appeared to be the only one in the house, and she only saw one car parked out front.

She put on the earmuffs, turned on the power for the amplification feature, and cranked the volume to high. With the window rolled down she could hear nearly every cricket in the county, along with the cars passing by and anything else making noise in the area.

At a little past nine-thirty an old pickup truck turned onto the drive. The sound of the large mud tires on the gravel road crunched into Sarah's earmuffs and she was forced to turn down the volume.

The vehicle parked in front of the house and she could see that Jim was the driver. She watched him as he climbed the stairs to the porch. He was holding a can of beer and gripped the handle on a twelve pack with the other hand. He stumbled a bit as he made it to the top step.

Janice had also heard the pickup pull up and threw the magazine on the coffee table. She rushed to the kitchen and stood in front of the stove stirring something in a pot.

As soon as the man entered the house, Jim started yelling at the woman about something. Sarah cranked the volume back to full and listened hard. She couldn't make out everything, but it sounded like the man was not happy about what she had prepared him for supper. For such a degenerate hillbilly he seemed to have a discerning palate, at least regarding fast food and chili.

The only voice that could be heard was Jim's, and Sarah could see from her binoculars that Janice had her back turned to the brute as he screamed at her. He moved in closer as the yelling intensified and eventually shoved the woman in the back. The spoon shot out of her hand and a spray of chili landed all over the wall behind the stove.

Sarah thought that her trap might be set after less than ten minutes, but Jim just threw up his hands and turned away. He walked out of her view somewhere near the back of the house. She could only see Janice now, who was using a towel to clean up the mess.

There was silence for a long while as Janice continued to stand at the stove, never looking back even once. She just stared at the pot of chili and out the side window. Every once in a while, she would wipe away a tear.

A creaking sound drew Sarah's attention and she swung the binoculars to the living room window where Jim had sat down in a recliner and turned on the TV. She could hear the faded sound of announcers calling a baseball game.

A few minutes later, Janice brought over a bowl of chili and sat it on a stand next to the chair. She walked to the fridge and pulled out a beer and sat it next to the bowl before heading back to the stove.

Jim picked up the bowl and swirled the spoon around sniffing the contents. He made a sour face but tried a spoonful anyway. It must have met his approval because he started eating.

He was a few bites in when he craned his neck around and yelled out a question. Sarah couldn't make out everything he said, but she was pretty sure she heard the word "cornbread."

Janice shook her head and muttered something. Her response caused Jim to jump up and knock the bowl of chili onto the floor. This led the man to rage even more as he looked at the mess all around him.

He was yelling at full volume now, so Sarah could make him out much clearer. "Now look what you made me do! First you serve me your nasty chili! Now, you don't even have the decency to make cornbread with it. What kind of wife are you?"

"I'm sorry. I didn't realize we were out of cornmeal until I started making dinner. I wanted it to be ready for you before you got home, and I thought crackers would be okay."

Janice had grabbed a large towel from the pantry and knelt down over the mess. She worked quickly trying to push all the chili into the bowl.

Jim reached down and grabbed her by the hair and pulled her head back to face him. "Woman, look at me when I am talking to you."

Janice reached back instinctively and grabbed his arm. Her nails dug deep into his wrist causing him to let go of her hair and grasp his now bleeding arm. Janice immediately recognized her mistake and turned to face him. She looked at him pleadingly and asked to see his injured arm.

Jim slapped her hard with the back of his hand. The blow hit the side of her face and knocked her to the ground and onto the mess of chili on the floor. She looked back in his direction just in time to see him reach a meaty hand around her neck. He was still in a rage and punched out with his right hand. She tried to turn her head to the side but couldn't move under his strong grip. His fist slammed into her nose causing it to erupt in blood.

The scene was jarring to Sarah, who had watched it all unfold through the binoculars. She was shaking with anger and nervous energy, as she yanked off the ear protection and picked up her phone. The number for the police tip line was programmed into her address book. She dialed it quickly and made a short report.

She knew that the man was violent and had been hurting his wife, but seeing it unfold in person was hard to stomach. She had dealt with plenty of violence in her life growing up in Kentucky, but she understood that was a different time. Not every woman had the experience and tools to protect themselves from men like Jim.

Now she had to wait, hoping that the call to the tip

line did not delay the response too long. It would have been faster to dial 911, but then her call would have been traceable and recorded.

She slipped the earmuffs on, picked the binoculars back up, and looked in through the window. Jim was now pacing around the room as Janice sat on her knees holding the towel to her face. The angry man was yelling obscenities at his wife, who could only sit and sob. Every time he got close to her she would flinch. This just spurred the bully on as he kept getting closer and closer with each pass.

Sarah felt like he was building up for another attack, which would be devastating to the broken Janice. Guilt was setting in, and she felt like she had to do something to keep the man from hurting his wife any further. She started the Jeep and looked back through the window. Jim paced back and forth a couple more times flailing his arms in the air. On the third pass he decided to kick his victim in the ribs causing her to crumple over on her side.

That was more than Sarah could stand. She had to do something. She turned on the headlights. Then she pulled the Jeep into reverse, yanked the wheel, and backed the vehicle up in an angle facing the house. She switched the headlights to bright, which sent a strong beam of light straight into the windows of the house.

The blinding light caused Jim to stop pacing and run to the living room window. He looked out trying to figure out where the light was coming from. He marched to the front door and threw it open. Still seeing nothing, he walked off the porch trying to get to the side of the white beams.

Once he was outside of the beam, Sarah could tell that Jim could see her Wrangler; which was parked about a forty yards from his position. He started to move that way, but the sound of a siren caught his attention. He looked up the highway and saw red and blue police lights that were quickly growing larger. He hesitated for a few seconds trying to figure out what was going on.

Something clicked in the man's head, and he quickly sprang into action. Jim ran into the house and started yelling out orders to his injured wife, who could barely move.

Sarah switched off the headlights and turned off the engine. The cops were very close now. She slipped the earmuffs back on. With the engine noise gone, she could catch Jim's panicked instructions.

"I think it's that old Fosterman woman. You know, the girl's grandma."

Janice was now on her knees trying hopelessly to clean up the mess around her. "Damn it. Would you knock that off? That's not going to help anything right now."

Jim dropped down to his knees and grabbed the woman's face and turned it toward him. "We have to protect our family, Janice. You can't say anything. If you do, those men will hunt you down like a dog, you understand me. Secrecy is the only thing holding this family together."

Janice was sobbing harder now, as she nodded. Jim kissed her on the forehead, a sentiment that looked very out of place to Sarah.

A second later, a marked car with two police officers pulled up in front of the house. The uniformed officers rushed to the front door with their weapons drawn. One of the officers banged hard on the door.

Jim let go of his wife, stood up, and walked over to the door. He turned the knob and pushed it open raising his hands above his head. The officers walked into the house and looked around. It was an ugly seen, made even grizzlier by the fact that Janice's bleeding nose had mixed with the pile of spilled chili covering the floor. Both Janice and Jim were covered in red blood and sauce, making it look even worse.

One officer quickly spun Jim around, patted him down, and placed handcuffs on him. He wasted no time removing the man from the house and guided him toward the police car.

The other officer helped Janice to a chair and grabbed a clean towel for her to hold on her nose. She protested when he told her he was going to call an ambulance. It took some convincing, but the officer relented when he could see that the bleeding had stopped.

Once Jim was tucked safely into the car, the other officer returned to the house. The pair took Janice's statement, along with pictures of her face and the messy floor. They tried again to convince her to go to the hospital, but she continued to refuse. After about fifteen minutes, they left the house with Jim staring out the backseat window.

Janice watched from the front porch as the car

pulled away and began crying. Sarah was standing outside of the Jeep now, and she could see the lady plainly enough from her position even without the binoculars. She wasn't sure if the woman was crying out of relief, fear, or true sadness. Whatever the case, she felt pity for the poor woman.

Sarah was about to get back in the Jeep when she saw Janice start to walk toward her. She panicked for a moment, not sure what to do. The woman posed no real threat to her, so she decided to stay put and see what she had to say.

Janice reached the cattle gate and grabbed onto the cold metal bars. "I know you're hurting over the loss of your granddaughter. But you have no idea what you've just done."

"I'm just trying to help both of our families, Janice. That man is a monster."

"He may be a monster, but there are even bigger monsters out there. He was the only one keeping my family safe. I would have taken a hundred beatings from that man to save my daughter."

Janice turned and started to talk away. She got a few steps before turning her head back. "Go home, Missus Fosterman. Go back to your family. There's nothing else you can do here now."

Sarah looked at her blankly, not knowing how to respond. She had considered that there might be other victims, but never once did she think that there could be other monsters.

She climbed back into the Wrangler and sat quietly, then began to cry. She had no idea what any of this meant. She had only wanted to keep her boys safe; to stop them from making life altering choices. Now she may have altered another family's life in a very dark way.

An Easy Win

The next morning, the district attorney was thrilled to see that Jim Powers' name was at the top of his case list. The public had been outraged when he could not secure a conviction on the man for killing Katie. The whole ordeal had been a huge embarrassment for everyone involved.

He knew that an assault and battery conviction wouldn't completely right the wrong, but it would put the man behind bars for a while and keep the negative stories out of the paper.

He spoke to the two arresting officers who painted a horrible picture of the scene. They both said that there was blood everywhere, and Janice had been punched, kicked, and slapped.

The only problem was that Janice did not want to press charges or testify against the man. He knew he didn't need her to get a conviction, but it would make things more complicated.

If she were to take the stand, he could likely get the man put away for at least fifteen years. But a trial without her support would water down his case. She would sit in the courtroom with pretty makeup and look like a loving wife. He would have to rely on police testimony and pictures of the scene to get a conviction.

He really didn't want to go through any of that. Not with this man, and not with the mayor and public breathing down his neck. He looked through the sentencing statutes and came up with a range of numbers he was confident would work. Then he entered the county lockup holding room where Jim and his lawyer were sitting.

After fifteen minutes of threats and potential outcomes, the young DA walked out with a smile on his face. He walked down the hall and called his clerk to have her start drawing up the paperwork.

"He agreed to an eight year sentence. It isn't real justice, but at least it keeps the bastard off the street for a few years. Write it up and send over the paperwork."

Temporary Reprieve

The entire Fosterman family sat around the table. It was mostly silent as no one knew what to say. Lucas had received the call from the district attorney about an hour ago, and he called the family meeting to break the news.

Lucas looked sad, but Sarah could tell he was also relieved. He had been worried about what the boys might be planning, and the fact that Jim was now in prison took all those options off the table.

The boys on the other hand looked aggravated by the news. Not just because of the short sentence, but because they felt cheated out of having an opportunity to make the man pay.

Their reaction was all Sarah needed to know that she had done the right thing. Now she just hoped time would help them move on with their lives. It would not be easy dealing with Katie's loss, especially now that they didn't have something to focus their anger toward.

Jim would get out in eight years or less, and they might have to deal with another round of tough decisions. But for now, they would have to focus on each other and moving past the hurt.

Later that night, she got ready for bed and kissed Lucas goodnight. He quickly fell fast asleep, but she could not stop thinking about what Janice had said to her in front of that gate.

She decided to get up and go into the kitchen. She grabbed the bottle of rye whiskey and poured herself a sip. Her father's memory had started her on this path, and maybe it would help her to figure out what to do next.

After taking a swig, she was no closer to discovering an answer. But one thing was clear. She was going to find a way to make things right.

CANCER – PART 1

"The bad news is nothing lasts forever. The good news is nothing lasts forever."

– J. Cole

The Diagnosis

Sarah Blackstone sat alone in the doctor's office shifting back and forth in the uncomfortable chair. She had been waiting for ten minutes for Doctor Gorman to arrive. The anticipation was beginning to weigh on her.

She had read nearly every internet article she could find about breast cancer, and of course, her mind always dove deep into the worst case scenarios. She wasn't even certain that she had cancer. The lump she had found on her breast last month might be nothing more than scar tissue or some other benign growth.

After finding the lump, she scheduled an appointment with her gynecologist who scheduled a mammogram. The test came back showing results that concerned her doctor. He ordered a full blood panel and sent her to the hospital to get an MRI. She had seen the looks on the technician's face during the MRI, and she was fairly certain that they had found something unpleasant. She tried to engage them in conversation to ask questions, but they just kept deflecting by saying that Doctor Gorman would be the one to determine the results.

She had discovered the lump nearly three weeks ago and had not told Lucas or anyone else about the abnormality, the doctor's appointments, or any of the additional tests. She had hoped to spare him and the rest of her family more sadness. They were all still dealing with the murder of Katie, and there was no need to give them more to worry about until she had a definitive diagnosis.

She continued to run scenarios through her head until the doctor came into the office. He was a stocky man in his late fifties with gray hair and thick glasses. He smiled at her as he walked in and set her chart on his desk. He sat down facing her, clasped his hands together, and paused for a second before speaking.

Sarah had the sudden urge to kick the man in order to force him to get it over with, but she just returned the smile and waited as patiently as she could.

"Sarah, I'm afraid the news is not what we had hoped."

"I see. Well, how bad is it then?"

"I really hoped you would have brought your husband or someone else with you today. Is there anyone we can call?"

"It will be fine Doctor Gorman. I'm prepared for the worst. You know all that my family has gone through this year. I can handle anything you have to say."

The doctor sat back in his chair and took a deep breath. "You have metastatic breast cancer. It is a stage four and advanced form of breast cancer."

"If it's stage four, that means it must have spread to other areas of my body?"

"That's correct. The MRI shows that it has spread to the lymph nodes in your left armpit. We will have to do another, more intensive round of testing to get a better idea of how far the cancer has spread, but there is a possibility that it may also be in your lungs."

"Well, I'm assuming that the first step will be surgery, followed by radiation and chemotherapy."

"That's correct. I'm hoping to schedule you for a double mastectomy as soon as possible. I'm having my office check for options, now."

On cue, the phone buzzed and Doctor Gorman picked it up. He listened for a moment to the female voice on the other end of the line, then told the lady to hold. "There is an opening on Monday morning at eight for the MRI, and we can schedule the surgery for that Friday. That would give you the weekend to speak with your family and make preparations. You would be in the hospital for at least four, maybe five days."

Sarah nodded her head almost subconsciously. She thought she was ready to hear bad news, but she was suddenly having a problem processing the information. She understood that terms metastatic and stage four likely meant her case was fatal.

She listened to the doctor as he rattled off orders to his assistant. He read off a list of medications and forms and gave other instructions.

Sarah lost focus on the conversation as she thought about her family. A knot started to form in her stomach, and she started visualizing the conversation with Lucas, then her children and her grandson, then the rest of her family members and friends.

She realized that Doctor Gorman was talking to her. "We're just going to have to take this one step at a time, Sarah. First is the surgery, then we will work with the radiologist and oncologist to determine the best course of treatment from there."

Sarah continued nodding her head. She knew she was missing a lot of details, but she got the basics. All she understood right now was that she had cancer, very bad cancer, and that she was going to have surgery next week.

The doctor's assistant came into the office carrying a sack of pills and a clipboard. The doctor stood up and told Sarah that he would see her again on Monday as he watched her follow the lady out of the office.

Sarah was led into a side office and sat down at a small table. The assistant went over a list of instructions and forms. Sarah filled out a few forms before looking over the instructions. She could tell that every detail had been covered in writing, so she didn't read most of the details. She had a strong desire to get out of the office as soon as possible.

The assistant finally stopped talking and told Sarah that she could finish the rest of the forms at home and bring them with her to the hospital on Monday. Sarah forced a smile as she left the office and walked to her Jeep Wrangler.

She wasted no time starting the vehicle and pulling out of the parking lot. She drove a few minutes before pulling into the parking lot of a supermarket. She placed the Jeep in park and laid her head on the steering wheel.

She began crying. How the hell was she going to tell Lucas about all of this? How the hell was she going to tell everyone?

FIRE IN THE BELLY

"Appear weak when you are strong, and strong when you are weak."

— SunTzu, The Art of War

Fall 1961

The Long Flight

Sarah's heart pounded as she sat in the tenth row of a Pan American Boeing 707. They had just started to taxi toward the runway, and she was anxious to leave the Seattle airport. Looking at her reflection in the window, she couldn't tell if the streaks of water were from her tears or the light rain that was starting to fall.

In answer, a soft-spoken older lady in the next seat handed her a tissue. "Oh, honey, are you alright?"

"Thank you. I'm fine." Sarah wiped her eyes and sat back in her seat. But she wasn't fine. Her father was in the hospital with his second massive heart attack in under a month. She could only hope that he would still be alive by the time she got back home to Kentucky.

She sat back in the seat and closed her eyes. It had been a whirlwind of a week, and she wasn't sure how to feel. She was sad and scared about her father, but she was also buzzing after an amazing few days she had spent with a man she never expected to meet.

She had met Lucas Fosterman just a few days ago while at a tradeshow that she had attended on her father's behalf. She was at the show to meet with whiskey and liquor companies looking to acquire the oak barrels that her family produced at the Blackstone

Oak Barrel Company.

She hadn't expected to meet a man on the trip, in fact she was trying to avoid even the appearance of impropriety while on the business venture. She had been intrigued by the young Marine when she met him at a rooftop bar at the hotel she was staying. Somehow he had convinced her to accompany him on a drive around the Puget Sound area the next day.

The trip around the beautiful Washington countryside had been quite the adventure filled with drinking, arm wrestling, great food, and even a short period of romance. But that adventure ended abruptly when she learned about her father's heart attack. She only had a few minutes to say goodbye to Lucas before jumping into a taxi and heading to the airport.

If things had been different, she would have likely stayed at least another day with the interesting man. Now, she was left with a folded piece of paper containing his name and a military address to some strange city in Japan. She doubted it would turn into anything, but at least it gave her mind a peaceful thought to settle on instead of worrying about the worst case scenarios she might soon be facing with her father.

Back in Kentucky

The plane landed in Nashville at a little past four in the afternoon. Sarah was waiting for her bag when her eldest brother, Victor, found her in the baggage claim area. He smiled at her, but she could tell it was forced.

The eighteen-year-old looked out of place in the modern airport wearing his overalls and a red t-shirt. He had on a floppy hat and a pack of Beech-Nut chewing tobacco hung out of his center pocket.

She hugged him tight, doing her best not to cry. She wiped away a tear before pulling away. He was looking down trying to keep from crying himself. She didn't want to ask him about her father. Not yet anyway. They would have plenty of time to discuss that on the two and half hour drive to Bloomfield.

Her bag was pushed through the baggage hold, and Victor grabbed it. They left the airport and found the green International Harvester R-100 pickup sitting in the parking lot. Sarah was relieved to be back on solid ground and hoped they could get to the hospital before dark.

On the drive north into central Kentucky, Victor updated Sarah on her father's condition. He had started having problems breathing a few days ago, just after Sarah left for Seattle. He was too stubborn to go back to the hospital like their mother kept telling him. He resisted until two days ago, when the pain in his chest became unbearable. When they got to the hospital, the doctor said he was having a heart attack that was even worse than the first one he suffered a month ago.

They had done some sort of experimental surgery on him to fix the blockage, but he had only woken up once since the surgery and even that was only for a few minutes. The news worried Sarah because she knew her father did not do well with lying in a hospital. If there was any possible way he could get out of there, he would make it happen the second he was able to make his escape.

To make matters worse, Victor told her that Old Man Cinder was making a play on their customers. The competition for selling charred oak barrels had gotten stiffer over the past decade, and Cinder was her father's biggest competitor in their region. He had heard about her father's first heart attack about a month ago and started seeding doubt with the bourbon producers in the area. As soon as word of her father's second attack spread, Cinder made sure to go to all the Blackstone Company's competitors to tell them the news.

She knew that a great deal of her father's customers would stay loyal to the company no matter what happened. Her family had been providing barrels to customers in the area since prohibition ended nearly three decades ago. But about a third of the companies they supplied to had only been in business a few years, and they would not be as loyal.

A drop in business of even twenty percent would be devastating because they had recently taken out a bank loan to build a new warehouse and modernize their forges. If she could just talk to her father he would know what to do. She was certain he already had a plan for how to deal with the problem. He always had a solution.

It was nearly dawn when they pulled into the hospital parking lot. Sarah pretended to check her hair in the mirror as they parked and made sure her eyes were dry with no signs of sadness. She wanted to look strong for her mom and her little brother and sister. And even stronger for her father.

Changing of the Guard

Sarah and Victor walked into the critical care waiting room and found their mother, sister, and brother sitting on a bench. Their heads were hanging low, and it was clear that they all had been crying.

Brian was twelve and he was wearing overalls and a red t-shirt like his older brother. Paula was fourteen but looked much older, wearing blue jeans and a gray shirt, always the tomboy.

They all jumped up when they saw their older siblings arrive and grabbed them around their necks. Mother started crying again as she told them the latest news. The doctors were back in the room working on him now. He had suffered another attack, which was worse now that his chest had been recently opened. It would be nearly impossible for the doctors to perform CPR on him.

They all waited for someone to come out knowing there was little chance of survival. After a few minutes, the doctor came out and spoke to the family. "Elwood has experienced another heart attack, and this one was even worse than the one he had earlier.

He is awake now, but he is having a lot of trouble breathing. I honestly don't know how much time he has left, but I don't believe it will be much longer. He's asked for you Sarah."

Sarah looked around at the rest of her family. She didn't want to go back in that room alone, but she also didn't want to go against her father's wishes. If he had used his strength to ask for her, then she had no choice but to go.

She followed the doctor through the double doors and he led her to the curtain shrouded bed where he dad was laying. "Mister Blackstone is through those curtains."

Sarah pushed the light fabric aside and walked up to the side of the bed. Her father looked smaller than normal laying on the bed. He was pale and had tubes sticking out of his nose and arm. She dried her eyes and steadied herself before grabbing his hand.

"Daddy, it's Sarah. I'm here."

Elwood turned his head slightly and opened his eyes about halfway. He looked at his daughter and smiled. He started to talk, but the sound was muffled and low. Sarah leaned in so she could hear him.

"I'm going to need you to be strong, girl. You're in charge now. I know it's not fair, but you're the only one that can keep the business going and take care of the family."

"Daddy, don't talk that way. This is no time to be talking about business."

He turned his head further in her direction and opened his eyes wider. "Now listen to me, Sarah.

Your brother is still young and hot headed, and your mother has always spent her time caring for the family. You're the only one who can do this now. Old Man Cinder is gunning for us, and you're going to have to fight him back right away if there's any hope of keeping the company going."

"Alright Daddy, I'll take care of it."

"No girl, you promise me. Promise me you will protect the family legacy and take care of those little ones."

"I promise, Daddy. I will, I promise."

"Good then. Now go get your momma and the others. I want to talk to them while I still can. But if I have another blasted attack, you keep them away. I told the doctor I was done with any of that CPR nonsense. If the Good Lord is calling me home, then that's his business."

Sarah nodded and kissed him on the forehead. "I love you, Daddy."

She returned to the waiting room and told them all that he was ready to see them. It would need to be a quick visit because he needed his rest. The family followed her back to the room and they took turns at the bedside. Mother was last, and Sarah had to eventually pull her away as the doctors came in to check on him.

As they left his bedside, they could see more doctors gathering around him and the sounds of hushed panic. She knew this was the end for her father, but she made sure that everyone continued walking forward. She didn't want them to see what was happening.

As they reached the waiting room, she took a second to let her mother sit down and looked at each of them with loving eyes. Her mother looked at her, wiping her nose. "He's going to pull through this isn't he, Sarah?"

Sarah looked back at the double doors. The doctor was now standing there with a blank look on his face. She nodded at him knowingly and held her hand up to let him know that she would deliver the news.

Taking care of the family was her responsibility now.

The Funeral

Sarah wasted no time arranging the funeral. She wanted to make sure they honored their father, but they also needed to restore confidence in the distillers in the area that the business was still running. She couldn't set meetings until everyone had a chance to pay their respects, and she knew Cinder was taking advantage of every minute the Blackstone Barrel Company was shut down.

Her father had died on Thursday, and the funeral was held that Saturday. Nearly everyone within fifty miles of Bloomfield showed up for the service. There was standing room only at the back of the church; which was lined with liquor distributors, moonshiners, farmers, and distillery workers. The majority of the gruff collection of men avoided sitting in the fancy wooden pews.

After the service, a potluck dinner was held in the backyard of the church. It was a warm sunny day, as the crowd of nearly three hundred walked around the grassy lawn eating off paper plates.

Sarah, her mother, and Victor stood in the corner as a line of visitors passed by offering their condolences. The two younger Blackstone siblings were spared the sad social convention as they sat at a table with their friends.

One by one, family members, friends, acquaintances, and customers shuffled through the line giving hugs and sharing their favorite stories about Elwood. It took nearly an hour for the family members and friends to pass through, which was a thankful reprieve for Sarah. By the time the line got to acquaintances and customers both her and her mother had become a bit numb to the sad stories and heartfelt platitudes.

Sarah could see that there were now only about forty people in line. At the center of that group was Old Man Cinder. She could see that he was not really waiting in line so much as he was working it, finding reasons to let people pass him by as he talked up another one of their loyal customers. She made note of every customer he talked to.

She didn't want to be disrespectful to her mother, so she refrained from talking business in the line, but she was certainly going to make an effort to speak to those people as soon as possible. As key customers came up and gave their condolences, she told them to please stay and have something to eat and she would find them later to say hello again before they left.

Once they got to the end of the line, Cinder came up and hugged her mother. It made Sarah's stomach turn, but she tried not to let it show. He whispered something to her, then approached Sarah and moved in for an embrace. She stepped back and held out her hand instead. After a short handshake, he asked if she might have time to talk in a little bit.

"Now Mister Cinder, I hope you're not trying to talk business at my father's funeral." She said in an uncomfortably loud voice.

"Not at all. I just want to extend an offer to help out in any way I can. I know how hard it can be to deal with the loss of such a vital part of your family and the cornerstone of your business. I'm here to help you and your customers."

"Don't you worry about us. We'll be just fine, Mister Cinder. And you certainly don't need to be worrying about our customers."

The awkward conversation drew a few odd looks, and Cinder shuffled his feet as he walked away. He looked back giving Sarah a crooked grin, then took his wife's arm and walked away.

Now that the line was finished and Cinder had left the area, she felt a sense of relief. She grabbed Victor and told him about what she had seen their rival doing in the line. His blood instantly started to boil, as he looked around for the old man. She grabbed his arm, spun him around, and started barking out orders.

"Go find Clement, Washburn, and Kilgore. You know those guys better than I do. Set up meetings with them early next week. The sooner the better. I'll get with any other customers I see here and start setting up meetings. We need to talk with everyone who's bought barrels from us in the last year."

The rest of the afternoon they spent time talking with every customer they could find. As expected, most of the older customers told them they would remain loyal no matter what. They had all been approached by Cinder already but had no intentions of changing vendors… as long as quality and delivery expectations continued to be met.

It was the newer customers that were in jeopardy. Cinder had used their father's first heart attack to approach those customers nearly a month ago to sow seeds of doubt and to offer deeply-discounted rates on future purchases. Sarah was able to set appointments with the two largest companies in that group, and even got one of them to tell her what type of discounts they were being offered.

After the funeral, Sarah and Victor returned to the company workshop and sat around a table talking over what they had learned. It was clear that things were going to get worse. They were going to have to work twice as hard to deliver the next month's orders of barrels ahead of schedule and without any defects. They were also going to have to match some discounts that may even mean losing money on orders.

Sarah sat back in her chair and stared up at the

large wooden sign that hung on their wrought iron gate that read Blackstone Oak Barrel Company in black charred letters. She thought about the promise she had made to her father. It was going to take a lot of work and a little luck for her to keep that promise.

Rallying the Troops

The next day Sarah arrived at the factory before daylight and fired up the primary forge. She started heating up stacks of metal bands that would serve as the hoops for the barrels. It was a tough and dirty job, but it was her favorite part of the process. She had hammered out nearly thirty bands before the first workers showed up.

By the time the full crew arrived at eight, there were nearly a hundred bands stacked in the bin. She shut off the forge and stood up on a finished barrel to address the group. She looked out over the small crew of a dozen men and four women.

"Thank you all for coming to the funeral this weekend. I know things haven't been easy the past several weeks. My father was the backbone of this company, and there is no way me or Victor or anyone is going to be able to replace him."

The group started nodding slowly, and a few mumbled yesses were heard.

"We may not have my daddy's experience, but we do have the legacy he built. We can't let his legacy go down in flames. We've all worked too hard to let that happen. Worked too damn hard to let someone like Old Man Cinder come in and take away what we have built."

Cheers started coming from the crewmembers and hammers clinked on metal and knocked on wood.

"We have to show every customer out there, every liquor distributor in the area, that the Blackstone legacy is still alive and well. Show them that this company continues to be ready to produce the best damn oak barrels in all of Kentucky!"

Cheers and hammering rang out throughout the shop as everyone rushed off to their stations. Sarah jumped off the barrel and turned to her brother. He smiled at her and grabbed a big stack of wood staves.

Sarah made sure to check in with every crewmember before heading to the bathroom in the back of the office to get cleaned up. She came out wearing a white t-shirt and blue overalls and carrying a clipboard.

She felt awkward as she made her way back through the shop and past the busy workers. One by one they each stopped to look at her for a second as she passed by. She got to the front where Victor was working on fitting a metal hoop around a ring of wooden staves.

He stopped for a second to eye her from head to toe. "Holy crap. You look just like Pa'."

"I figured it couldn't hurt to wear the company uniform while visiting customers."

She threw the clipboard into the old green truck before jumping in and firing up the inline six cylinder engine, ready to head out for her first appointment.

From High to Low

It had only been a week, but Sarah was feeling cautiously optimistic about keeping the company moving forward. They had filled all the open orders, and she had connected with all their biggest customers to reassure them that things were still on track.

She did have to give deeper discounts than she wanted to a few of the newer customers who had been approached by Cinder, and two customers had already committed to ordering from the old man. Luckily, Victor had been able to secure a large order with a new customer in Tennessee that more than made up for the loss.

It was as good a start as she could hope for given the circumstances. However, Sarah's good mood was quickly shaken the next Monday when one of her seasoned foremen, along with three workers, gave their notices. Cinder had moved from stealing customers to stealing workers.

The loss of four experienced craftsmen was a serious blow to their production capacity. Now she only had a week to replace the workers and a clipboard full of orders to fill. Victor suggested offering the men more money in an effort to keep them, but Sarah knew that would set a bad precedent. Instead, she had to be talked out of not firing the men immediately for their disloyalty. They needed all the capacity they could squeeze out that week.

By midweek, Sarah had to fire the men anyway when she caught them trying to recruit other workers to leave with them. This increased everyone's workload and cast a cloud of negativity over the remaining workforce.

Victor had to spend all his time in the workshop, and Sarah had to postpone a few meetings in order to help keep the forge crews on schedule. By Saturday, they had managed to fill all the orders, but it had come at a cost. The overtime hours had increased labor costs and several barrels had to be rejected for quality issues.

Victor walked into the office late that night to see Sarah sitting at her desk sorting through paperwork. She was covered in black coal dust and her hair was frazzled. He could see the stress on her face.

"The last truck just left. We filled all the orders for this week, but it took every barrel we had. That order for the new customer in Tennessee really put a strain on things."

"I know. We were so fixed on keeping customers that we overextended ourselves too much. We certainly can't keep going like this for much longer."

"It will get better. We just need to replace a few workers and increase the numbers a little each week."

"We also need to improve our quality control. I had to reject nearly a dozen barrels this week. That would have saved us most of the overtime right there."

"I know, but we can't fix it all tonight. Let's go home and get some sleep. We can come back after church tomorrow and go through the books."

Sarah shuffled the papers into a pile and reluctantly got up from the desk. The two of them headed out to the parking lot toward the old green truck. As they closed the large iron gate, they saw a puff of dust in the distance as a vehicle was racing up the gravel road in their direction. A minute later they could see the shiny grill of their shipping manager, Bill's, truck.

The tall wiry man pulled up beside them and hung out the window. "Luther's truck's on fire. He's down by the old mill."

Sarah jumped in with Bill and told Victor to follow them. That truck was carrying twenty barrels.

The Charred Remains

The firemen were already rolling up their hoses by the time Sarah and Bill arrived at the scene. The back end of the Ford truck's bed was a total loss. The fire had reached every piece of wood on the vehicle, including the wooden bed, sides, and tailgate. The entire load of twenty barrels had been reduced to a heaping pile of ash. The only parts that looked salvageable were the engine compartment and front of the cab.

They found Luther sitting on a rock at the side of the road with a bandage around his right hand and arm. He was an older black man with short curly gray hair and a smooth shaven face. He looked very grumpy.

Sarah gently pushed the fireman to the side and knelt down beside the old truck driver. "What happened, Luther?"

"It was the damndest thing. I was driving along and all the sudden I saw a ball of flame shooting up from the back of the truck. I know I didn't hit anything. I was just driving along on this here road and then it happened."

Sarah tightened the wrap on his arm and stood him up. "I want you to go with Bill now. He's going to take you to the doctor to get that looked at."

"I don't want to be a bother, Miss Sarah. I've already caused enough trouble."

"None of this is your fault, Luther. We can get another truck and make more barrels, but we only got one of you." She nodded to Bill who helped the driver to the truck.

The fire captain walked over holding a charred piece of wood the size and shape of a barrel stave that was wrapped in fabric. He sniffed the cloth and wrinkled his nose. "I'm pretty sure this is what started the fire. Smells like diesel fuel to me."

A flash of anger shot through Sarah as she looked at the makeshift torch. It was obvious that their shipment had been sabotaged. She was confident it wasn't anyone from the Blackstone company. All the vehicles they owned were gas powered, and they had coal forges.

There was only one operation in the area that used diesel, and that was Cinder Barrel Works. They used diesel powered tractors to make their local deliveries, and even their forge was powered by diesel fuel.

A rumbling sound caught Sarah's attention, and she saw Victor jump out of the cab of the burned delivery truck. "I think I can drive this thing back to the workshop. The engine and cab are still in decent shape, and there's enough rubber left on the tires to make it a few miles."

Sarah turned to the fire captain and pointed to the torch. "You mind if I take that with me?"

The captain handed her the chunk of wood. "I don't see why not, it was in your truck."

Sarah tossed the torch in the back of the International and jumped in the cab. "Captain, thank you for all your help today. Victor, I'll see you back at the house."

It took Victor a moment to realize what was happening. He lunged toward the truck as it sped away. "Sarah! Sarah! Don't you go and do something stupid!"

This Means War

The green truck screeched to a halt in front of Cinder Barrel Works and Sarah jumped out of the cab and grabbed the piece of wood from the back. She walked with long purposeful strides toward the office door, then pushed her way into the small room without knocking.

Old Man Cinder was sitting in a chair in the corner sipping on a jar of whiskey while his grandson, Coal, a behemoth of a man with a huge belly and shaggy beard leaned against the wall. Coal was covered in dirt and soot, and he had a handkerchief wrapped around his hand.

Sarah stood in the center of the room looking back and forth between the two men. She had prepared a speech on the drive over, but the sight of the two men smirking at her caused her blood to boil. She tossed the remains of the torch at Coal's shins, causing him to jump back out of the way to avoid being hit.

"I believe this belongs to you."

She stood there staring at the large man, who was easily four times her size.

Coal started to walk toward her puffing out his chest. Cinder held up his hand signaling for his grandson to stop. "Now there little Miss Blackstone, what has gotten you all worked up this afternoon?"

"You know damn well what has me worked up. Are you really that scared of one little girl that you have to start burning my shipments? I knew you were a son-of-a-bitch, but I had no idea that you were a low down, dishonorable son-of-a-bitch."

The insult caused Coal to clinch his fist and move in closer. Sarah wasn't about to back down, and she closed the gap between herself and the large man.

"Now there is no need for name calling, honey. I heard about your truck and the fire. I am real sorry about all that. This here is a real dangerous world and things like that happen. Now, if you need help filling those lost orders, you just let me know. I would be happy to talk to your customers about making things right."

"You stay away from my customers, old man. And stay away from my trucks and my employees. You think I'm weak because my daddy's gone. Well you're about to find out just how strong I am."

Coal was now hovering less than two feet away from her. Sarah dug her heels into the floor and pushed out with both hands. Her palms caught him just under his massive belly and she shoved hard. The motion caught the man off guard and he went tumbling backward and crashed hard against the wall.

Cinder stood up out of his chair after seeing his grandson fall into a heap. He looked up at the girl with wide, angry eyes.

"You picked a fight with the wrong little girl, mister."

Sarah marched out of the office and jumped into her truck. Rocks and dirt sprayed out as she peeled out of the driveway and back onto the road.

Dinner Time

The entire Blackstone family sat at the table for Sunday dinner. It was the first time they had all been together at the table since the funeral. Sarah and Victor had protested the mandatory family time saying they were too busy, but Mother insisted.

The meal was a quiet affair with no one wanting to say much about their days. The younger siblings had always been the quiet ones, which usually left Victor as the main entertainment. He was holding his tongue this evening for fear that he might say something about the fire. Sarah was also quiet, as she was still seething from her meeting with Cinder.

About halfway through the meal, Mother decided she was done with the silence. "I heard that one of the trucks caught on fire today."

Brian and Paula looked up from their plates with wide eyes. Sarah kicked Victor under the table and shot him a scolding look. "Don't look at me, I didn't say anything. Did you really think the rumor mill wasn't going to spread that news around?"

"I'm just glad Luther was alright. Did anyone else get hurt?"

"No, Mama, no one else got hurt. We just lost a load of barrels, and the truck was tore up pretty bad. We'll be okay." Sarah looked at Victor signaling for him to help with some words of reassurance.

"I should be able to fix that flatbed Ford tomorrow. It just burnt up the stakes and ruined most of the wood on the flatbed. We will also need to replace the back tires, but it should be ready to go after that."

"Luther can help you fix the wood parts in the morning, and I will go by the service station and fetch us some new tires."

"Now, I don't need to remind either of you that this is a good Christian family. I don't want either of you doing something that's going to bring shame on this house. Just because that Cinder clan is acting like heathens doesn't mean you get to in return."

"Yes, ma'am." Victor looked down at his plate, as everyone started eating again. Everyone but Mother. She kept looking at Sarah, waiting for a response.

Sarah looked up at her mother trying to think of something creative to say. She fully intended on responding in a very unchristian-like way. The look on her mother's face told her that she was not going to get away from the table without agreeing to lay down arms.

"Yes, ma'am." She finally said it in a small voice, hoping that maybe the softness of her words would negate her agreement. It didn't work.

"What was that young lady? I'm not sure the Lord heard you."

"Yes, ma'am." Sarah understood that the matter was now settled. She couldn't carry out any of the plans she had set in her mind to sabotage Cinder's operation. She had spent the entire day thinking of plenty of dirty tactics that would have more than sufficed as proper retaliation.

"Good then, after supper I have a small box of your daddy's things I want you and your brother to go through. It's just a few things he had in the bedroom and in his pockets."

The conversation picked up after the exchange, as Brian and Paula asked about a hundred questions about the fire. They didn't care that their older siblings were uncomfortable with the conversation.

The news was just too big for them to ignore.

The meal ended with a round of their mother's peach pie, and the young ones were assigned clean up duty. Mother handed Sarah the small box of her father's things. It contained his wallet, pocket watch, and his Swiss Army knife.

She handed the pocket watch to Victor. "He would want you to have this. Maybe it'll help you to make it to work on time."

He punched her in the arm and laughed. "Then Brian should get the knife. He's old enough to carry a pocket knife now."

Sarah went through the fat leather wallet and started pulling out the contents. It had a wad of money, which she set aside for Mother, and a stack of photos. The photos were all of the family including one of each child, one of the entire family, and one from his wedding day.

There were other assorted folded pieces of paper including some receipts and a bill for an order of steel that was set to arrive in a couple days. Lastly, she found a carefully folded piece of paper that she opened. The letters and numbers didn't look familiar to her. There were about fifty lines that looked like codes of some sort. Each line had BR in front of a number followed by what looked to be a date. She looked at the last two lines which read BR-8 10/28/61 and BR-12 11/4/61. The notes were in her father's handwriting, but she had no clue what they could mean.

She showed the paper to Victor who shook his

head, then she took the note to her mother. She looked at it for a long while but couldn't come up with an answer. Sarah folded the paper and stuck it in her pocket. Maybe she could find something at the office tomorrow that would give her a clue as to the meaning of the odd list.

Help From Above

The next morning Sarah stopped by the mechanic shop to pick up the tires before driving to the workshop. Victor and Luther were already fitting new wooden planks onto the flatbed when she pulled up.

After checking in with Bill to make sure everyone in the workshop was ready to start the day, she went to the office and sat at her father's old desk. She searched through all the drawers and sorted through the papers on his desk but found nothing that contained the letters BR.

She looked around the other areas of the office, including the filing cabinet that contained all the customer orders. She looked for any companies that had BR as their initials or at the start of their name. She found nothing.

Sitting back in the chair she racked her brain trying to figure out what the letters could represent. Maybe they stood for Blackstone, but why would her father use that for a code. Maybe the B stood for barrel, but that still didn't explain the R.

PARABLES OF SARAH BLACKSTONE

A knock on the door shook her from her thoughts. She knew it wasn't an employee, they never knocked. She opened the door to see Marty Bowman standing there. He was one of their largest customers, and the intended recipient of the barrels that had burned up in the fire.

"Good morning, Sarah. I wanted to come by and make sure everyone was alright. I heard about the fire."

"We are all good, Mister Bowman. Luckily, the fire started in the back and didn't hurt anyone or completely ruin the truck. But it did ruin your order of barrels."

"Well thank God for that."

"We have everyone working hard to replace those barrels, Mister Bowman."

"I appreciate that Sarah. But this couldn't have happened at a worst time. We have a large batch of sour mash ready to go to wood. We were really counting on those twenty barrels, and I was hoping to get at least another twenty more this week."

"I understand. I promise you we will get you as many barrels as we can, as soon as possible."

"I know you will. I really don't want to buy anything from Cinder, but I've got a mess of money tied up in this batch. I can wait at least a day to start pouring, but that is all I can push it. Bring me every barrel you can by then, but I will have to get the rest from Cinder."

"Thank you for working with us, Mister Bowman. We will get you every barrel we can make by then."

He nodded and headed out of the office, leaving Sarah alone to contemplate her options, which were few. They had barely kept up with demand over the past two weeks, and the loss of twenty barrels was at least two day's work. They were already working overtime, and the crews were starting to get worn down.

For now, all she could do was keep things moving forward. Maybe tonight she and Victor could think of some options, but for now she would continue researching the mysterious ledger.

Since the office hadn't yielded any results, she decided to go out to the workshop and see if she could find any clues there. She looked around the tool shed and at some of the larger pieces of equipment.

She decided to ask Bill, who was one of their employees. Maybe the B was in reference to him, although his last name was Johnson.

She found Bill standing next to the office door along with Luther. "Hey, Bill. I found a note of my father's that has a bunch of numbers on it that reference BR. Does that make any since to you?"

"Can't say that it does. I don't recall any customers with those initials."

"Well, thanks anyway. What can I do for you gentlemen?"

A loud banging sound drew Bill's attention, and he ran off to check on what had happened. Luther stepped up. "He was just trying to help me find you. I needed to get the keys to your truck. Victor and I need to go pick up a few more nuts and bolts at the hardware store."

"Sure thing, I think I left them on my desk." She walked into the office and Luther followed after her. He took off his hat as he entered the room out of habit.

"Miss Sarah." The formality of his address caught her off guard.

"Luther, what is it? You know you shouldn't be calling me miss. You were my daddy's oldest friend. I am the one who has to call you 'sir.'"

"Yes, well I don't mean to get into your business. And I don't want you to think I was listening in on your conversation or anything."

"Don't worry about any of that, Luther. You're just as much a part of this company as any of us. What are you trying say?"

"Well, I heard you asking Bill about Elwood's paper. I believe I may know what that paper is about."

At that moment Sarah realized that she should have probably started with Luther in the first place. He had been her father's best friend since they were little boys. Her father had even tried to make him a bigger part of the company over the years, but Luther never had much use for business or management. He was happy hauling barrels around and fixing whatever was broken.

She pulled the piece of paper out of her pocket and showed it to him. Luther had to hold the letter out at an arms-length to read the small type. "Yeah, it's what I thought. This is for the bootleg reserve."

"Bootleg reserve? Reserve what? I have never heard anything about that before."

"Well, you remember that old barn at the other end of the farm down by the creek?" He moved in closer and whispered. "You know, the one where we used to make moonshine when you were little?"

"I think so. The big red barn with the cellar."

"That's the one. Well, I helped Elwood put the old still in that cellar. Then we fixed up the barn a bit to keep out the weather."

"But what does that have to do with the ledger and the reserve?"

"Well over the years, every once in a while Elwood had me take the extra barrels that haven't been sold to the barn. He called it his Bootleg Reserve. He told me not to tell anyone about it cause he wanted to save them for emergencies."

Sarah's eyes widened. She couldn't believe that her father had kept this secret from them. It made sense to use the old barn. No one ever went out to the far end of the farm. Well, no one but Luther it appeared.

"Luther, how many barrels are in the old barn?"

"Well, you know I'm not certain. But it's a mess of 'em. I'm not good at adding things up, but I think this piece of paper should tell you. I have only taken barrels to the barn all this time. I've never taken any out. Elwood always marked down how many I took with me."

He handed the paper back to Sarah who started adding up the lines. "But Luther, that adds up to nearly three hundred."

"That sounds about right. I don't think we can fit much more in there."

She grabbed the keys off the desk and headed for the door. "We'll get your bolts later. Let's get Victor and go take a look at the barn."

The Mother Load

The large red barn looked weathered and old as they approached from the dirt road. Drawing closer, however, the barn looked to be in good structural shape. It stood tall without sagging in any areas, and many of the old rotted pieces of lumber had been replaced. The roof was also fitted with several new sheets of tin.

The sight of the old barn brought back memories for Sarah. She had spent many days in there watching her father and Luther brew up batches of moonshine, which they mixed with different fruits and spices before selling the jars to bootleggers who would sell the liquor outside of the state.

Back then moonshining was illegal but it was mostly just frowned upon by the authorities. The police normally only got involved when a bad batch poisoned people or when shiners got brave enough to open speakeasies to sell their products.

Elwood and Luther were a relatively small operation, and they had grown up with the sheriff and most of the deputies in the county. Plus, the fact that their products were sold out of state helped to minimize conflicts with other moonshiners in the area. This allowed them to run a successful still out of the barn for nearly twenty years.

The men had started making liquor during the prohibition era, and the operation was their main source of income until the mid-1930's. When the ban on alcohol ended in 1933 and liquor became readily available, their sales rapidly declined.

Elwood had anticipated that the change in laws would eventually mean an end to their moonshining business, so he spent whatever extra money he could scrounge up building a large woodshop on the other end of the farm located closer to the more visible highway.

His original plan was to build furniture, but that all changed when a friend of his obtained a license to legally distill bourbon. His friend needed oak barrels to age the whiskey, and there weren't many barrel makers in the region. Elwood got his first order in 1935, and it was enough to convince him to start making barrels full time.

Luther continued running the still on his own for a while, but a change in sheriff and tougher moonshining laws made running illegal stills a dangerous gamble. Elwood eventually convinced him to hide away the still and come to work with him at the barrel company.

As Luther started to open the barn's heavy roller doors, the smell of charred oak wafted through the air. The door rolled past Victor first, who stood frozen with his mouth gaped open. Sarah kicked at him to continue helping to push on the large doors.

Once the door was fully open Sarah could see what had caused Victor to pause. The entire barn was stacked full of barrels. There were five racks of barrels stacked three high. Sarah had counted up the barrels on her father's ledger, but she hadn't really believed there would be nearly three hundred barrels hidden away in the barn.

They both started walking up and down the rows inspecting the barrels. They were all pristine and ready to be sold.

Victor started counting the rows as quickly as he could. After ten minutes of counting he ran up to Sarah and Luther.

"There are over two hundred fifty barrels in here. I lost count after that." He was smiling broadly. "How the hell did Daddy keep this hidden from us?"

"Apparently, he had some help from an old friend." Sarah looked over at Luther.

"I just did as I was told. You know Elwood, he was always planning for the worst."

"Well gentlemen, Daddy's planning has really saved our bacon this time. We can fill Mister Bowman's order and then some. Let's go get you boys some bolts so you can fix that truck and start making deliveries."

"That sounds good to me," Victor said still shaking his head in disbelief. "But this time I'm going to ride shotgun, and I mean that literally. Remind me to pick up a couple boxes of twelve gauge shells when we get to the hardware store."

Ahead of Schedule

The repairs to the burned delivery truck were made by late afternoon, and the two men also performed maintenance on the company's other delivery truck. The Chevy flatbed was a bit smaller than the Ford, but they would need all the capacity they could get to deliver all the orders by tomorrow.

They didn't want to waste any time showing their loyal customers that the company was back to full strength. Plus, the faster they filled the orders, the more it would refute all the negative rumors Cinder had been spreading about their inability to keep up with demand.

Sarah and Victor decided to keep the barn a secret from most of the company workers because they wanted them to stay focused on producing as many barrels as possible. With the continued demand in the area, they would never run out of people wanting to buy quality products. Plus, they didn't want to completely clean out the secret store of extra barrels.

The only other person in the shop that was let in on the secret was Bill, since as shop manager he was responsible for keeping the daily count. He would have suspected something if they were able to magically fill a few large orders without pulling from his inventory numbers.

Sarah drove Bill out to the old barn in the Chevy flatbed, where Victor and Ted were nearly finished loading the Ford with a double stack of barrels. Bill's eyes went wide when he saw the full truckload of barrels. His eyes got even bigger when he saw the racks full of completed barrels.

"I always wondered what Elwood did with those extra barrels he took each month. I just thought he was giving them out as sales samples or replacing damaged goods or something. That is a lot of extra stock."

"We have enough to fill every open order and still keep back about a two hundred barrels. We should only take what we need and leave the rest in reserve. When we get caught back up with production, then we can start replenishing the bootleg reserve."

"That is what the BR stood for. It makes sense now. Elwood always joked that he might have to break into the bootleg whenever I told him that production was down. I just thought he was talking about drinking moonshine."

They helped Victor and Luther finish loading the Ford, then all four of them made quick work of loading the Chevy. Once both trucks were strapped down, they were ready to make their delivery to Mister Bowman.

Victor handed Bill a shotgun and a box of shells. "No one even knows we are out here, so I don't expect any trouble on the road. But we can't take any chances after the last ambush, especially since we have to drive by Cinder's place on the way."

Bill nodded and loaded three shells into the Remington and got into the passenger seat of the Chevy. Sarah started the truck and waited for Victor to ready his shotgun before he jumped into the Ford. Luther headed out first, and Sarah followed close behind.

The Bowman Distillery was about forty minutes away, and they passed by the Cinder Barrel Works at about the halfway point. As luck would have it Cinder and Coal were standing outside the office when the two trucks drove by. Victor made sure to flash his shotgun out the window so that they could see that their shipments were now protected during transport.

Coal bowed his head not making eye contact as Sarah waved out the window. Cinder narrowed his eyes and stared at the full loads. He was no doubt trying to count up the total quantity of barrels that he wouldn't be selling.

They arrived at the Bowman Distillery before noon. The warehouse manager was excited to see two full loads of barrels pull up and grabbed five men to come out and help with the unloading. Sarah went to the office to deliver the invoice.

"Good morning, Mister Bowman," she said to the owner as he stood up to greet her.

"Good morning, Sarah. Well, I'll be a roasted hog, is that two truckloads of barrels I see out there?"

"We have forty barrels for you this morning, and I can have another twenty for you this afternoon if you want."

"Well, hell yes. That is exactly how many I need for this batch. It looks like I won't have to buy any barrels from that old cuss after all."

"No, sir. And you just let me know if you need any more and I'll have Luther drive them over straight away."

By the time Sarah finished her business in the office, the men had already unloaded both trucks. She smiled at the manager and let him know they would be back in a couple hours with another truckload.

The Spoils of Victory

By the end of the week, the Blackstone Oak Barrel Company had filled every order on the books, and even a few extra ones once customers were certain that the company was able to accommodate their needs.

They had driven past Cinder's company well over a dozen times during the week, and the old man became madder and madder with each pass. By Friday, he had stopped counting the amount of barrels on the loads, and just sat in his rocking chair glaring at the shotgun riders.

They had also been able to keep the workshop running at top efficiency throughout week, and the extra revenues allowed them to increase overtime hours, which boosted morale. In the end, they only had to pull out half the bootleg reserve, which left a hundred and fifty barrels in the barn as emergency stock.

Sarah went to the metal supply store on Friday afternoon to order more sheets for cutting the bands they needed. With the added production, they were now running low on raw materials. As she pulled up to the metal yard, she saw Paul standing out front talking to a young man getting ready to cut some steel rods.

Paul was a friend of hers from high school. He had always been sweet on her, but he was a little too shy for her liking. Still, she considered him a good friend.

"Good morning, Sarah. How are things going for you today?"

"Going well, Paul. And how is your mamma and your sister?"

"They are doing good. Mamma is planning to bring by a couple pies to your house tonight. You know in honor of your daddy and all. I was real sad to hear about Elwood. He was a good man. I'm going to miss seeing him around here."

"Thank you for that. And thank your mamma for the pies. I wanted to see how many plates you had in stock."

"Well, we don't have a lot because all the supplies are being taken up by the war effort. We have one pallet left in the back, and I am not sure we are going to get another load in quite some time."

"Well, we will definitely take all you've got. But that won't last more than a week or so."

Sarah's disappointment must have shown on her face. "Why don't you come around to the back and let me show you something."

She followed Paul around to the back of the yard where she could see ten pallets of shiny steel sheets.

"We got a load of this in before the shortages started. It is galvanized steel. It costs a little more than the iron sheets, but this stuff is much better. It will hold up to corrosion and should bend a lot easier than iron. But it's still plenty strong."

"It sure looks shiny. I bet it would look nice wrapped around the barrels."

"If you want some of this, you should get it soon. We probably won't be getting any more of this or anything else for a few months. I know Old Man Cinder will be around next week trying to scrounge up all the metal he can."

"Well, we have to have steel. I'll take every pallet of this galvanized stuff you've got in the yard, as well as the iron sheets. And let me know when you get another truckload in. I'll put a deposit on it today, so that you can have it delivered straight to our workshop."

Paul smiled at her. "I guess Cinder will have to start hunting in the junkyards to find something to ring up his barrels. Serves him right for what he did to your truck."

Sarah nodded and followed him into the office to do the paperwork. She knew that buying all the steel in the yard would crush her rival.

Her mother may not approve of the tactic, but she knew it was the right business decision. Besides, she had to ensure that her workshop stayed busy throughout the shortages, and this would secure them enough steel to make it through the next six months and beyond.

Hollow Victory

The next month was very productive for the Blackstone Company as they continued to pump out orders at increased capacity. At the end of that month, they were even able to produce an extra twenty barrels to help start replenishing the reserve. They also signed up five new distillery customers and hired four new employees to replace the crew that had walked away at the beginning of their troubles.

The new galvanized steel bands were a big hit with the liquor makers who liked the polished look they gave the barrels. The workers also liked the new metal because it was easier to cut and bend into bands. The extra cost of the sheets was offset by the reduced labor needed during fabrication, so they didn't have to increase their prices.

Victor had convinced Sarah that they needed to get deliveries out faster, so she went out and purchased a large used flatbed that could haul forty barrels in one load. It was an older Dodge with low miles that Paul at the metal yard didn't need anymore, and he made her a great deal on the one-ton truck.

Sarah was sitting in the office when she heard a knock at the door, followed by Bill walking in. He normally didn't knock unless he had a customer or some other visitor waiting outside. "Sarah, you have a visitor wanting to meet with you."

She stood up and looked curiously at Bill who looked like he was keeping a secret. He closed the door behind him and moved in closer. "It's Old Man Cinder. He actually asked if I could check on your availability and all. He was almost... well, polite about it."

Sarah sat back down at her desk and rubbed her temple. She knew that they had been putting a dent in his business over the past month, but she didn't think that a few weeks of increased competition would hurt the man enough to come to her with hat in hand. The old barrel maker had been in business nearly as long as her father, so he had weathered worse than a few low selling weeks.

Something more had to be going on, but there was only one way she was going to find out. "Well, send him in. There is no reason for us to be impolite at this point."

"Yes, ma'am. But I will be right outside the door if you need anything."

"It will be fine, Bill. Besides, I keep a snake pistol in the top drawer to handle the vipers."

He smiled and nodded as he walked out of the office. A few minutes later Cinder appeared in the doorway wearing his trademark blue overalls and green shirt. He held his head high, but he looked older than the last time they had met face-to-face.

"Good morning, Sarah. You guys have really ramped up your operation since the last time I was around here."

"My father added on to the workshop buildings about a year before he died, and we are still building it out little by little."

"I saw that yard full of steel on the way in. I had a feeling that was where all the extra steel ended up. Young Paul always was a little sweet on you."

Sarah could sense the bitterness in his tone, and she dropped the polite smile. "Just good timing Cinder, nothing more. He had a full shipment of some new sheets, and I took a risk on buying a couple truckloads."

"I meant no offense. Money always talks louder than sugar any day. You definitely got my goat on that one. But I am not here to talk about that."

"Well, have a seat then. What is it you want to talk about?"

Cinder sat down in a wooden chair. He looked uncomfortable sitting in the small chair. He appeared to be wrestling with how to proceed. He looked grumpy, like always. But there was something underlying his countenance that betrayed his gruff exterior.

He pursed his lips ready to talk, but the words wouldn't come out. He was fighting back some emotion that Sarah couldn't place.

She sat silently for a few moments before deciding to stand up and walk over to the small cupboard next to the sink. She pulled out two glasses and grabbed a bottle off the shelf. It was some rye whiskey that her father and Luther had made many years ago. They still had a couple cases of the last bootleg batch they had ever made together.

She poured two glasses half-full and handed one to Cinder. He took a sip, and it was clear he was impressed. "This is the finest rye I've ever tasted. Is this some of Elwood and Luther's old stuff?"

"It is. We don't have much of it left, but I know he would have poured you a glass if he were still here."

The gesture struck a chord with the surly old-timer and tears started welling up in his eyes. "I really do miss the old days. Life seemed simpler when we were bootlegging moonshine."

Sarah took a drink, pulled up a chair next to Cinder, and sat down beside him.

"I'm alone now, Sarah. Coal left last month for the Army. His buddy got drafted, and he said he didn't feel right not signing up with him to go to that blasted place. You know my son died four years ago, and Coal was the only family I had left to help me run the company. I just don't have the heart for it anymore."

He took another sip of whiskey and wiped away a tear. Sarah decided it best to keep quiet a bit longer.

"It's just me and Reba now, and her health ain't that good. She can barely get out of the house anymore. I got a dozen mouths to feed at the shop, and it gets harder every week with the steel shortages and damn gas prices."

Sarah stood up and grabbed the bottle of rye and poured him another glass. "You've seen all this before. You survived the big flood. A tornado took out half your building a few years ago. Even the liquor tax laws didn't slow you down all that much."

"I know. I know. I guess I'm just tired. I must be. I've never blubbered on like this before. I guess I always thought this company would be my legacy.

But if Coal doesn't care about any of that, I guess I shouldn't either."

"Well, what else are you going to do? You've been in the liquor business all your life. You and my daddy started making barrels at about the same time."

"Marty Bowman has offered to buy my workshop, land and all. He quoted me a fair price, and I reckon I'm going to take it."

Sarah wasn't sure how to react to the news. She decided to swallow the rest of her glass to buy herself a little time.

Cinder stood up and handed her the glass. "Thank you for the drink. And thanks to the Blackstone family for years of spirited competition. Why don't you and Victor come over next week and pick through the bones?

"I'll give you a good price on whatever would be of use to you. I'd also appreciate it if you would think about hiring my guys. I know there is some bad blood with a few of them, but they are family men and there aren't a lot of good options out there right now."

Sarah stood up and set the glasses on the desk. She turned around and shook his hand. "We will offer all of them jobs here, if they want to work. And we will pay invoice price for any raw materials you have on hand."

He smiled and nodded before heading out the door. He passed Victor on his way out and patted the young man on the shoulder.

Victor walked into the office wearing a confused look. "He actually looked pleasant today. What was that all about?"

"Sit down, dear brother. We have a lot to figure out."

Closing Shop

A week later Sarah, Victor, and Bill arrived at the Cinder Barrel Works driving their two largest stake bed trucks. Cinder was sitting in the rocking chair outside his office already nursing a mason jar full of whiskey.

He stood up when they walked up to the porch and waved in the window of the workshop for his yard manager to come out. The tall, gangly manager came outside wearing blue overalls and holding a stack of papers.

"I believe you all know Baxster. He has been my manager for twenty years or so. He can show you around the shop and let you pick out what might be of interest to you. We have to get everything cleaned out by the end of the week. After that, whatever is left is included in the sale."

A plump middle-aged black woman with thick black hair came out while the old man was talking and stood next to Baxster. "And this is Sue. She has all the info on the boys we have working in the shop. We have eight regulars, one driver, and two youngsters that fill in part-time when needed."

Sarah nodded. "Victor, why don't you go with Baxster? We'll buy all the raw materials you have, and we might be able to give you a decent offer on some of the equipment and tools if you can wait a few months for payment."

Cinder waved his hand back and forth. "Don't worry about any of that stuff. I am sure ya'll will be fair enough. Whatever you don't buy will probably be sold off as scrap."

"Bill, you can sit with Sue and figure out all the personnel stuff. I told Cinder we would offer everyone a job, and I would like to match their pay if possible."

"Alright, Miss Sarah. You want to work on it in the office, Miss Sue?"

Sue giggled at being called "miss" and led him into the office.

Cinder sat back down in his rocking chair and took another sip of whiskey. Sarah sat down in the chair next to him and they looked out at the green barley field across the road. The old man grabbed an empty jar and used his handkerchief to clean it out. He poured it half-full of whiskey and handed it to his companion. "It isn't as good as Elwood's rye, but Marty Bowman's bourbon is about the best of what they try to pass off as whiskey these days."

"Thank you, Mister Cinder."

"Now don't go back to being all formal now, Sarah. Just call me Cinder. Too many men around these parts have a problem with a young woman running a business. Calling them that haven't earned it mister just makes them feel like they got their fat boots on your neck. You've got a legacy to protect now for two generations of barrel makers."

"It's not going to be same without you around to push us anymore. Are you sure you're ready to give all this up?"

"I'm sure. I slept better this week than I have in a long time. Marty gave me a good price for this place, and I'm happy that the boys will still have a good place to work. That's enough for me."

Sarah sat back in the rocker and sipped on her jar. The pair rocked for a while sitting in comfortable silence enjoying the breeze. Finishing his drink, Cinder stood up and walked in the office. He came back out a few minutes later and tossed a set of keys to Sarah.

"Those are for the big Dodge flatbed around back. I'll have Baxster sign it over to you. Coal never should have done such a corn-brained thing, and I shouldn't have been such a fool in defending him. This should help make amends for all that."

"You don't have to do that, Cinder. We were able to salvage the truck."

"Nonsense. It will make me feel better. Besides, what am I going to do with a big clunker like that?"

"Well, if you ever need to haul anything just let me know and I'll send someone out."

He nodded and sat back in his rocking chair uncorking a new bottle. It took Bill and Sue about an hour to sort through all the personnel. They came out and said that six of the workers had agreed to join the Blackstone Company, including Baxster and Sue. The others had either found work with local distilleries or were ready to retire.

Victor came out and asked Bill if he could drive the truck around back and help start loading the wood staves and other tools. He said they would probably fill up at least three truckloads with everything. Sarah threw the keys to the Dodge truck to Victor and told him she would be back in a minute to help with the loading.

By late afternoon, all three trucks were loaded with nearly every piece of wood, steel, and scrap of raw material in the building. They had even managed to load up a small forge and two furnaces along with four large boxes of tools. Bill headed out with the largest load first, followed by Victor in the Dodge. Sarah drove the Ford out of the workshop and pulled up in front of the porch.

Cinder stood up and locked the door to his office. He turned as Sarah reached the porch and handed her one of the rocking chairs. He grabbed the other and started walking toward his truck. He placed the chair gently in the back and Sarah tucked the other one in beside it.

Sarah reached into the Ford and pulled out two bottles of her father's rye whiskey and handed them to Cinder along with a check. "This should cover all the raw materials and about half the equipment. I'll get you another check next month if that works for you?"

He looked at the check. "These bottles of whiskey will take care of the rest. Besides, I'd rather have an open favor if you don't mind? I may need it sometime down the road and that's more valuable to me than money at this point in my life."

Sarah understood that owing a favor to a man like Cinder was a really big deal. The last favor that was called in for her father involved a dead body and few bags of lye. She hesitated a second before holding out her hand.

Cinder shook it and nodded before jumping in his old Chevy. Sarah watched as he drove down the dirt road. She could see the dust cloud grow smaller, and she wondered what would become of their old competitor.

She got in the Ford and started back to the workshop. There was a lot of work to do now that the Blackstone Oak Barrel Company was the only game in town.

CANCER – PART 2

"Enjoy the little things in life, for one day you may look back and realize they were the big things."

– Robert Brault

Delivering the News

Telling Lucas about her cancer diagnosis was heartbreaking. She knew it would be. But even knowing how he would react couldn't prepare her for seeing him go through the pain. He had always been a strong man, but he simply wasn't prepared to handle a new round of gut-wrenching news.

She watched as her husband went through all five stages of grief in one afternoon. He started with denial, mainly because he hadn't been through the testing processes with her. He questioned the diagnosis and asked every question that she had already gone over with multiple doctors.

He became angry at her for shutting him out for the past several weeks, but he moved past anger quickly once he understood her motivations.

He lingered on bargaining to the point of annoyance, as he tried to figure out how he could manipulate a different outcome. Maybe if they changed her diet. Maybe if they tried some alternative treatments. He even talked about flying to the Mayo Clinic to see if there were any experimental treatments available.

Depression set in at dinner time, and they both shed tears as they talked about how they were going to break the news to the boys. They thought about waiting a few days, but Sarah argued against that path. She had already held the secret for too long, and she didn't want the boys to resent their father for also keeping the news from them.

By that night, Lucas had clearly moved on to acceptance. He stayed up through the night poring through her medical records and test results. He searched the internet to learn about double mastectomies, targeted radiation, and the various forms of chemotherapy available to treat breast cancer. He understood that there was little chance of remission in her case, but there was enough of a chance that they could hope for at least a year or more of life and possibly a miracle. At least it was something to cling to, and some ray of hope to offer the boys.

Sarah woke the next morning to find him sleeping at his desk with the glow of his monitor still shining. She woke him up and convinced him to lay down in bed for a few hours while she prepared brunch.

He woke up at ten and took a shower. By the time he entered the kitchen, Mark and Paul were already sitting at the kitchen table eating. Sarah had considered asking Mark's wife Lisa and her grandson Tyler to join them, but she knew it was going to be hard enough to deliver the news to her sons. Having her grandson there was just too much to bear.

Lucas walked in and sat at the table. He was happy to see his sons laughing and eating heartily. They waited until the meal was finished before starting the conversation.

Their reactions were nearly identical to Lucas' from the day before. They couldn't believe the news and were furious that their mother had gone through all the testing alone. It broke Sarah's heart to see her grown children cry. She had only seen Mark cry three times as a man and that was after the births of his children, Tyler and Katie and after they discovered Katie's body. She had never seen Paul cry, at least not since he was a little boy.

By the afternoon, Sarah escaped to the bedroom, using a headache as an excuse to remove herself from the scene. Lucas understood that his wife had reached her limit and told the boys it was time to leave. They were also left in charge of telling others in the family about the news. There was no need for Sarah to have to go through any of that again.

Sarah prepared herself for bed and sat down in her reading chair in the bedroom. She looked out the window at the pear tree in the back yard. The large tree had been a favorite of hers for years. She laughed as she looked at the big juicy pears hanging from the drooping limbs. She knew Lucas hated that damn tree. It was so hard to mow around once the fruit started falling, but he never complained to her about it.

She knew he would probably cut that tree down as soon as she was gone. At least that would be one thing he could look forward to in all this sadness.

BULLIES, BEASTS, AND BROKEN BONES

"Wrath, when entertained by mere mortals, is nothing more than a self-righteous need for revenge and fuel for bad tempers."

– Author Unknown

Summer 1951

Big Fat Bully

Sarah Fosterman was pedaling as fast as her eleven-year-old legs would move as she powered her yellow Schwinn bicycle down the gravel road. Close behind her, Milly Beeman was doing her best to overtake her wiry competitor.

They had been racing for about a quarter mile, and Sarah's calves were burning. Her rusty old bike was no match for Milly's new Firestone Cruiser. Sarah's only advantage was the fact that she was a seasoned farm girl, while Milly was a much softer city girl.

The road straightened out for the final stretch to the finish and Sarah gritted her teeth to get a little extra power. She pulled away from Milly a bit more as they approached the mud puddle they had designated as the finish line. She crossed the finish and stopped just past the puddle and turned to see Milly, red faced and peddling hard.

Behind Milly was a rusty pickup truck filled with a group of teenage boys. Two boys sat in the cab, while another three were hanging out the back. As Milly approached the finish line the truck caught up with her and swerved like it was going to run her over.

The sudden movement of the vehicle startled the girl, and she pulled her handlebars hard to the right causing the bike to flip end over end. Poor Milly was thrown into the center of the mud puddle, landing hard on her side as the pink bike fell on top of her.

Sarah looked at the driver and saw that it was Claud Stimpson, a good-for-nothing bully that had been terrorizing her and her brother for years. She yelled at him and pumped her fist in the air as he passed. The other boys in the truck hooped and hollered at the brutish act and laughed even harder at Sarah's angry chastisement.

Sarah ran over and pulled the bike off of Milly and helped her roll out of the puddle. Milly screamed out in pain as she rolled, grabbing onto the lower part of her left leg. Sarah looked at the leg and could tell by the awkward bend that it was definitely broken. There was no way the little girl was going to be able to ride or walk back home.

Sarah pulled her bike to the side and made sure Milly was out of road. She told her to wait there while she went to find help, then jumped on her bike and sped off toward her house.

She took a shortcut through a field which cut her travel time down to ten minutes and jumped off the bike at the front of the house and ran inside. There was no one home. She knew her father would be working at his workshop today, but her mother should be around. She rushed from room to room but found no one in the house. She passed by the kitchen table when she noticed a note: *Went to the market. Be back in an hour.*

Sarah hesitated for a minute trying to figure out what to do next. Milly's house was four miles in the opposite direction. She was pretty sure that her mother was home, but she hated the idea of leaving Milly out on that road for much longer.

Sarah ran out and grabbed her bike. She was about to pedal off, when she noticed her grandpa's Jeep Willys Model MC. He had purchased the new Jeep a year ago, just a few short months before he passed away. It was now her father's prized possession, and the family's favorite reminder of her grandpa.

She had driven the fancy vehicle a few times in the fields with her father, but he would not be happy about her taking it out on her own. Sarah decided that this was an emergency, and he would just have to understand the severity of the situation.

She ran over to the Jeep and positioned her feet on the peddles. She pushed down on the clutch, but her short legs could barely reach far enough to engage the transmission. She managed to put the vehicle in gear and started the engine. She pushed down on the gas pedal and let out the clutch. The vehicle lurched forward and stalled out. She grumbled at herself and started the process again. This time, she was able to get the vehicle moving forward without stalling.

It was an effort for her to move the steering wheel as she muscled it around the driveway and onto the gravel road. She managed to shift into second gear, but in doing so she had to duck below the windshield to push in the clutch. She ran off the road during the process, clipping the right fender on a tree branch. Her father was not going to be happy about that dent.

Now that the Jeep was moving at a higher rate of

speed, the steering became easier. She managed to drive the three miles back to where Milly was sitting by the side of the road holding onto her broken leg. Sarah pulled the Jeep up beside her and jumped out to help her up. Milly cried out a few times as they worked together to get her into the passenger seat.

Sarah grabbed Milly's bike and threw it in the back of the vehicle. She got back into the driver's seat and stalled out again before managing to get on the road again. Milly's house was only a few miles down the road, and Sarah had to pull with all her strength to make the turn into the driveway. However, she wasn't able to pull on the steering wheel and work the pedals at the same time, which caused the Jeep to race forward. The vehicle was now speeding toward a tree, and Sarah let go of the wheel and smashed down hard on the peddles. The brakes engaged, throwing both girls forward into the dash. Even with the sudden stop, the right bumper of the Jeep slammed into the tree.

Milly cried out in pain as she fell back into her seat grabbing her leg. Sarah's head slammed into the steering wheel, and a large gash appeared on her forehead.

The sound of the vehicle hitting the tree and Milly's screams had alerted everyone in the house to their arrival. Milly's mother and father came running out. They rushed over to see the wrecked Jeep and two injured girls. Milly pointed to her broken leg as Sarah wiped away the blood that was now trickling into her eyes.

Milly's mother held her hands to her head in surprise. "Good heavens. What the devil happened to you girls?"

Sarah climbed out of the driver's chair and looked up at Milly's bewildered mother. She took a couple steps forward ready to explain, but felt the world swirl around her as she fell to the ground.

Band-Aids and Bad Decisions

Sarah woke up in a warm bed with white sheets pillowed all around her. She could hear the beeping of machines and saw the shadows of people walking around her in hospital uniforms. Her head pounded, and she sat up on her elbows and could see her mother sitting at her side.

"Oh honey, are you alright? You scared the tarnation out of me."

"I'm sorry, Momma. I didn't know what else to do. Milly broke her leg, and she was all alone. Is she okay?"

"I know, honey. We can sort all that out later. Milly is fine now."

Sarah saw her father push his way into the curtain surrounding the bed. She could see the panic on his face as he entered.

"Is she okay? The nurse said she hit her head and passed out." Her father walked in wearing his normal overalls and red t-shirt. He bent down to look at the three inch curved gash on her forehead. There were several stitches holding everything together.

"I'm fine, Daddy."

His panic faded, quickly followed by a spark of anger. "What the devil were you thinking, girl? You could have gotten yourself killed."

"I know, Daddy. I shouldn't have taken grandpa's Jeep. I messed it all up pretty good."

"Don't worry about the Jeep, girl. I'm just upset that I didn't do a better job teaching you how to drive a stick shift." He smiled at her and leaned down to give her a hug.

"Elwood, don't you go encouraging her now. She could have really gotten hurt."

"She was just being a good Christian girl like you taught her to be and all." He winked at Sarah as he rubbed his wife's back. "The nurse said we could take you home after the doctor has a look at you."

A few minutes later the doctor walked in and looked over the injury. He said that Sarah had a concussion and that she would need to stay in bed for the next couple of days. Sarah didn't like the idea of sitting in bed for that long, but at least she was able to go home that night.

As they left the hospital, they stopped by Milly's room to see that she had already been fitted for a cast. Milly's father was so grateful for Sarah's rescue effort that he insisted on paying to fix the damages to the Jeep.

Milly's cast covered her foot to just below her hip, and there was no way she was going to fit in the back of her parent's Buick Roadmaster. Elwood offered to take her home, and they all waited until Milly's family was done checking her out of the hospital.

Elwood lifted Milly into the bed of his pickup, and the two girls rode together in the back of the truck.

They dropped Milly off at her house, and Sarah promised to come see her as soon as her mother released her from her mandated bed rest.

Bed Rest and Battle Plans

Sarah was forced to stay in her bed for the next two days, only getting up to leave her bedroom to go to the bathroom. She slept through the first day, but the second was unbearably boring. Her mother finally let her get up from bed to come to dinner the morning of the third day, and she spent the rest of the day being made fun of by her younger brother and younger sister for looking like a mummy with the large bandage wrapped around her head.

By day four the bandaged was reduced to a few large band-aides, and she was allowed to go outside for a little while. Her mother still would not let her leave the yard or ride her bike, but at least she could sit on the porch swing and enjoy the fresh air. She waited until her father got home that night, but even he wasn't able to convince the warden to release her from home confinement.

It wasn't until the end of the week that she was finally given permission to ride her bike over to Milly's house. Milly was sitting on her front porch swing with her leg sticking straight out. It was a hilarious sight and Sarah laughed as she walked up the stairs.

Milly joined in on the laughter as Sarah sat down beside her. They sat in silence for a few minutes looking over each other's injuries. Then Sarah got serious. "I think we should pay those stupid boys back for being big bullies… especially Claud Stimpson. He is the worst."

"I agree, but how are we going to take on a bunch of boys."

"Don't you worry about that. I have an idea that will make them think twice about picking on a couple of country girls."

Milly smiled at her friend. She knew Sarah well enough to know that she wasn't one to issue idle threats. If she said had a plan, then it was almost a guarantee that it was going to be carried out. The two girls scooted in closer together as Sarah laid out her plan.

"Well, the first thing we have to do is find a bunch of the critter traps stored away in my daddy's shed."

Making Preparations

After two weeks, Milly went back to the doctor and got fitted for a different cast. The new model was more of an oversized boot, which allowed her to move around much quicker. She hated that she couldn't ride her bike, but Sarah's father helped the girls rig up a wooden platform on the back of Sarah's. It was an awkward setup that forced the passenger to sit backwards, but it at least gave Milly a way to get around other than hobbling on her crutches.

The girls convinced Milly's parents to let her stay the night at Sarah's that Saturday, and the two girls started working on their plan to get back at the bullies. They started by rooting through the old run down shed behind the house. Sarah was a girl on a mission as she dug through the heaps of wood planks and scrap metal looking for the wire cage traps. It took nearly an hour to find four traps that were in good enough shape to use. Three of the traps were large enough to catch raccoons or opossums. The fourth one was smaller and only fit to catch squirrels and rabbits.

Sarah was determined to get the traps set that night, but her mother called the girls in once it got dark outside and scolded them for getting so filthy in the shed. They were both forced to take baths that night to be ready for church the next morning.

The girls sat together during the Sunday service and whispered back and forth about what they were going to use to bait the traps. As soon as they were released from lunch in the church yard, the two girls rushed back to Sarah's house where they quickly changed out of their Sunday dresses and into their play clothes.

They went to the shed to collect the traps and carried them out to the woods in two trips. They wanted to be sure to get them far enough away from the house so that they wouldn't be noticed by Sarah's father or uncovered by her younger siblings. This proved to be harder than they expected due to Milly's impaired mobility. Sarah offered to complete the task on her own, but Milly wouldn't hear of it. She was too excited by the prospect of catching wild animals in the small cages. Living most of her life in the city, she had only ever seen rats caught in snap traps, but those were always dead when captured. To see a live animal in a cage would be quite the adventure.

They set the traps about fifty feet apart and baited them with pieces of fruit and smudges of peanut butter. They covered them with bits of leaves and branches for camouflage and headed back to the house.

They had just cleared the woods when the rest of the family came pulling up to the house. Sarah's mother got out of the truck and waved them over. "Milly, your momma wants you to head on back home. Sarah, why don't you run inside and get Milly's dress for her and your daddy will give her a ride to her house now."

Sarah ran inside and grabbed Milly's things and jumped into the truck and scooted over to the middle. Milly climbed into the cab and they headed down the gravel road.

After dropping off Milly, Elwood asked Sarah about what the girls had been up to that afternoon. Sarah just giggled a little and said they hadn't done much of anything.

He gave her a crooked smile as he looked down at

her mud covered boots and saw the black grime on her hands from rooting around in the shed. He wasn't sure what they had been up to, but it certainly wasn't "nothing."

Wild Beasts

The next day, the girls weren't able to get together until the early afternoon. They immediately headed out to the woods to check the traps. Sarah was disappointed by the results. Two of the traps were empty of bait, and a third hadn't been touched at all. The small trap had caught one cotton-tailed rabbit, which was very exciting to Milly. Sarah let her look at the small creature for a while before letting it escape back into the wild.

Their plan would take at least three decent sized animals, and a fluffy bunny was not going to get the job done. Sarah pulled two apples out of her pocket, and used her pocket knife to cut them in half. This time, she used some baling twine to tie the bait to the traps, hoping that securing larger pieces of bait to the cages would give them a better chance of catching something.

By the time they got back from their trip in the woods, it was already time to take Milly back home. The round trip on Sarah's bike with Milly onboard made the four-mile trip take a lot longer than usual.

During their ride, they were passed by Claud and his band of ruffians. They stopped long enough to laugh at poor Milly as she hung on tight to the platform and made faces at them.

The next day, Sarah was able to finish her chores early in the day, so she was able to pick up Milly just after lunch. The two girls headed into the woods to check the traps. To their delight, all three of the large traps had caught an animal. There were two fat raccoons and one opossum sitting in the cages. The small cage was still empty, but that didn't matter, the larger animals were all they needed.

Sarah pulled the apples out of her pocket and cut them into pieces. She stuck the pieces into the cages to feed the wild beasts. She didn't like the idea of keeping them locked up for too long, but they had to wait at least another day or two before they could put the rest of their plan into motion.

The girls headed back to the house so they could start getting things ready.

Learning the Hard Way

The next day the girls did a double share of their chores, in an effort to appease their parents. They planned to work hard over the next two days in order to ask to spend all Friday afternoon together.

Sarah's mother was always busy with her younger siblings, and Milly's mom was still nursing her new baby brother. This meant that the ladies never had much of a chance to see each other outside of church. They decided to take a risk and ask to stay at each other's houses in order to have all of Friday evening to carry out their plan. It was a gamble but they felt it was worth it to carry out their mission.

Sarah picked up Milly at five in the afternoon. Both girls were still dirty from working all day, but they were also excited to check on the animals that were still locked in the cages.

Once they got to the woods, Sarah took off the drawstring bag she had brought with her and removed a couple of apples. She started cutting up pieces of fruit, while Milly pulled out a few slices of bread she had brought from home. They had to be careful when sliding the food through the small holes in the cages because the animals were not happy about being cooped up in their prisons for so long.

Sarah took out three tin bowls from her bag and closed it back up. She told Milly she was going to go down to the creek to fill the bowls with water. Milly nodded and continued slipping pieces of bread into the cages.

The creek was located down in a gully, and it took Sarah a while to get to the water and climb back up the steep incline. She was almost back to the area where the traps were sitting when she saw Milly several feet away leaning over the small cage that had remained empty over the past couple days.

"Oh Sarah, it looks like we caught a poor little kitty cat in this small cage. I think I should let it out."

Sarah sped up her pace and tried to get a look at the cage. She reached the first large cage with a raccoon in it and set down the bowls of water.

"That's funny. It is making a weird growling noise. I've never heard a cat do that."

Sarah's eyes went wide and she started running toward her friend. "Get away from that thing, Milly."

As she drew closer, Sarah's nose told her that it was too late. A pungent smell similar to a mixture of sulfur, rotten onions, and burned rubber overtook her senses. Milly cried out as she turned away from the trap.

"That kitty just peed on me!"

"That's no cat, Milly. It's a skunk! Move away from there before it gets you again."

Just then a second stream of liquid hit the little girl, soaking the back of her shorts and covering her cast. The smell was so strong that it made their eyes water.

Milly hobbled as quickly as she could, trying desperately to get away from the foul beast and pungent odor. It didn't take her long to realize that the odor was not coming from the animal, but from her.

She got to Sarah, who helped her sit down. The girls held their noses as they tried hard to breathe. Holding their noses only made matters worse because they had to open their mouths to get air. This meant they could now taste the horrible fumes.

Sarah had been around dogs that had been tagged by skunks, so she was a little more prepared for the smell. She closed her eyes and waited for her nose to adjust to the foul odor.

For Milly, the sensation was overwhelming and she threw up a couple of times. She had smelled the scent from skunks hit on the road before, but the full spray from a live animal was a much different matter. The intensity was magnified by at least ten fold.

The two girls sat for fifteen minutes as tears and snot poured out of their bodies. The smell was still intense, but they had acclimated to it a bit more. Milly wiped her nose on her sleeve and turned to Sarah.

"What are we going to do now? I can't go home like this?"

"We should head to my house. My momma will know what to do. We will just tell them we came across a skunk and it sprayed you. There's nothing uncommon about that."

Milly nodded as she stood up. She hated the idea of trudging back to the house stinking so bad, but there wasn't another option.

The girls walked out of the woods and up the road to Sarah's house. Even before they got to the door, Sarah's mother was standing outside holding her nose.

"My Lord, girls. What have you gotten yourselves into now?"

Scrub, Scrub, Scrub

Cleaning the skunk smell off Milly took several hours. Luckily, there was a horse trough behind Sarah's house that the younger kids used as a makeshift swimming pool. Sarah's mother added a few pots of boiling water to the trough along with some laundry detergent. Sarah jumped in the water and helped Milly with the scrubbing.

Elwood came home just in time to laugh at the hilarious scene. Milly's leg was wrapped in a plastic garbage bag and hung over the side of the trough while Sarah propped the girl up and lathered her up with soap. He held his nose as he came in closer to inspect the situation.

"Good heavens, girls. You must have really riled that critter up to get a spray like that."

"Elwood, what are we going to do with this poor girl. Her cast is covered in that stuff, and we can't wash that off."

"Well, I better go see if I can fetch her parents. Why don't you call Doc Goldman and tell him we will be along in a little while to see about getting that cast replaced. I don't think anyone wants to keep that thing around any longer than we have to."

Elwood jumped in his truck and headed out. Sarah and her mother continued scrubbing on Milly as the younger Blackstone kids watched from the window inside the house. Victor was laughing so hard that he fell off the windowsill.

Elwood returned a few minutes later with Milly's parents Paula and Jimmy, and they came around back to see their daughter covered in soap and smelling horrible.

Her mother clasped her hands over her mouth in shock, while her father just started laughing. Milly wiped the soap away from her eyes. She looked just pitiful in the large wash tub with her leg sticking over the side.

Sarah and Paula lifted Milly out of the trough, while the two fathers tipped it over and emptied it out. They filled the trough with fresh water and started the cleaning process again. After a second cleaning, the smell had subsided a little, but it was still strong enough to burn everyone's eyes.

Elwood and Jimmy lifted Milly into Elwood's pickup. Both of their mother's climbed into the cab and Jimmy climbed into the back with the girls as they all headed into town.

Once they got to the doctor's office, Elwood suggested everyone wait in the truck while he went inside to fetch Doc Goldman. There was no need to subject everyone else in the waiting room to the horrible stench.

A few minutes later, the gray haired doctor came outside and approached the vehicle. He paused for a second when the smell reached his nostrils, but kept moving forward. He looked at the young lady with her leg wrapped in a garbage bag and smiled at her.

"Don't worry, honey, we'll get you out of that stinky cast and fix you back up."

He turned back to the two men and tried to stifle his laughter. "Elwood, can you and Jimmy lift her out of the truck and sit her on the curb over there?"

The men lifted Milly out and sat her down on the sidewalk. By that time, a small crowd had started to gather around to see what the fuss was all about. The smell was strong enough to keep people back, but Milly's face turned red anyway.

The doctor took out a pair of cutters and laid them by his side. He unwrapped the plastic around the girl's leg and started pulling it down. The smell intensified once the bag was opened, and everyone in the small crowd took several steps backwards and started holding their noses.

The doctor's eyes began to water up, and he turned his head away for a second as he tossed the bag to the side. He grabbed the cutters and made quick work of removing the cast. Once finished, he handed the pieces to Milly's father and asked him to throw them in the trash.

The doctor turned to Milly's mother. "Alright, there is a shower in the back of my office that we can use to clean off that leg. I'll go through the main entrance and open up the back door. You can enter through there. One of you men can carry the poor girl around."

Elwood picked up Milly and started walking around the back of the building, along with Paula and Sarah. The doctor met them at the back door and handed Sarah a handful of supplies.

"Here is some baking soda and hydrogen peroxide. Mix this together and coat her down with it. Then wash it off and do it again. Once she has cleaned all that stuff off, use the soap to clean her up again."

The girls headed into the shower and Sarah mixed the ingredients together as she was told and used a sponge to coat Milly down with the pasty mixture. After just the first coat, the smell reduced a great deal. The second coat nearly eliminated it altogether.

Milly's skin was pink from the applications, but she insisted that Sarah use the rest of the mixture to coat her down a third time. She then slathered on the soap and washed herself a few more times.

Milly's mother came into the bathroom and handed her daughter a gown to wear and scooped up her dirty clothes and placed them in a sack. By the time the girls left the shower, they both had wrinkly fingers and pink faces from the hot water.

The doctor took Milly into the exam room and inspected her leg. He told her she didn't have to be fitted for a new cast and instead slipped a brace onto her leg that looked like a large black boot. He tightened the straps and told her she would need to continue using one crutch to keep weight off the leg, but she should be able to lightly walk on it over the next week.

Milly was excited to finally be done with the ugly and itchy cast, and the new boot felt like a feather on her leg. She hobbled out of the exam room and nodded at Sarah as she rounded the corner.

The two girls exchanged smiles as they linked arms. They knew that Milly's new mobility would help them carry out their mission much easier.

The Setup

It took Sarah a whole day to wash out the skunk smell from all the areas of her house that had been infected. Her parents made her do most of the work by herself, which included cleaning out the horse trough and her father's truck. It also meant washing the smelly clothes several times in the creek before bringing them back to wash them again in the wash tub outside the house with fresh soap and water.

She was soaking wet by the time she finished her chores, but she was happy to be done with the awful tasks. Throughout every minute of her work she used the anger to fire he desire to get back at Claud Stimpson. It had now been over three weeks since he had run Milly off the road, but she was madder than ever at the bully and his band of hooligans.

It was late afternoon when Milly's mother dropped her off at Sarah's house. She got out of the car and kissed her mother before slinging a sack over her back. She was moving much faster now that her leg was held together with a simple brace. She used only one crutch and was able to walk at nearly full speed with her new setup.

Sarah met her at the front of the driveway and took her sack from her. She stored it behind some bushes out of sight and led her into the house.

"Did she buy it?"

"She did. She is taking the baby to her sister's house in Louisville for the night, so she won't be back for two days. What about your parents?"

"They gave me permission to stay the night at your house tonight. I told them we would be camping outside in your backyard tonight, so they wouldn't ask questions about the bags."

The two girls felt secure in their stories as they

headed up to the house. Elwood met them at the door as they walked up. He put on his ball cap as he grabbed his keys and a sack dinner. Sarah knew he was heading out to work on the far end of the farm.

Her father spent his days working at his workshop making furniture and oak barrels for some of the distilleries in the area. In the afternoons, he would sometimes meet up with his friend Bill down at an old red barn where they kept a moonshine still in the cellar. Bill did most of the shining, now that her father had a business to run, but Elwood still helped with the bottling and loading from time to time.

He reached down to give her a hug as he left. "You girls stay away from skunks tonight. I've had about all of that smell I can take."

The girls laughed and nodded as he walked away. They rushed into the house and headed to Sarah's room where they began packing. Sarah grabbed a large gunny sack and stuffed in a blanket and a canteen of water. She also tossed in some pieces of fruit and a bag filled with beef jerky. Last she pulled two Baby Ruth's out of her top dresser drawer and placed them in the bag. She cinched up the top and carried it out to the living room.

They found Sarah's mother sitting on a rocking chair knitting on a scarf. They said their good-byes as quickly as they could; not wanting to raise any suspicions.

"Sarah, you be home tomorrow before nine. Your daddy needs you to help him sort out the barrel staves. And Milly, tell your momma thank you for the apple pie she brought by for us. She didn't have to do that."

"Yes, Missus Blackstone, I will. She just wanted to thank you all for helping to get me to the doctor."

"Good bye, Momma." Sarah kissed her mother and headed to the door.

"That is quite the bag you've got there Sarah."

"Just a blanket and stuff for sleeping outside."

"Okay, but just make sure you bring it back safe and sound. Your grandma made that quilt for you."

"I will, Momma."

The girls pushed out of the door and headed for the bushes where Milly's bag was stashed. They hopped on Sarah's bike and started down the driveway, turning onto the gravel road. They got about halfway to Milly's house before turning left down the logging road that led into the woods where they had set the traps. Once they got to a bend in the road, they hid the bike behind a cedar tree and walked the rest of the way into the clearing near the traps.

Sarah rushed around and checked to make sure that the traps were still full. The two raccoons were still as angry as ever, but they calmed a bit when she walked up. They were starting to get used to seeing her in the afternoons for their daily feedings. The opossum didn't look as lively. She stuck a few pieces of apple into the cage, and the opossum slowly lumbered up to the fruit and started eating.

The skunk was still in the small cage, and she fed it using a long stick. She hated dealing with the foul beast, but it was now the key to carrying out their plan to extract revenge. It took her a couple tries, but she finally fed the beast three large chunks of apple.

The two girls backed away from the cages and sat down on a stump. They snacked on the jerky and fruit while going over their plan of attack. Once the sun started to set, Sarah pulled out the blanket and the two girls huddled together and covered up.

Now they just had to wait a few hours for everyone to go to sleep before they started their mission.

Covert Operations

Sarah couldn't be sure what time it was, but the full moon sitting directly overhead told her it was at least midnight by now. She shook Milly lightly to wake her up, as she rubbed her eyes and looked up at the bright moon.

"I think we should head out now. It will take us at least an hour to get these cages down to the cabin. Maybe longer if we decide to take the skunk with us."

Milly's nose crinkled up at the thought of dealing with the skunk. Sarah picked up the two cages containing the heavier raccoons. The muscles in her skinny arms drew tight as she lifted both cages and started walking back toward the logging road. Each trap with a raccoon weighed about twenty pounds, and the angry critters banging against the sides made the effort even harder.

It took all the strength she could muster to carry the cages the quarter mile to the end of the logging road. Milly followed close behind her carrying the lighter opossum, while shuffling along in her boot supported by a single crutch.

The girls set the cages down at the edge of the road and looked down the hill at the run-down wood cabin situated at the bottom of the hill next to the river. They still had about a thousand feet to go, but it would be easier traveling downhill.

Sarah turned around and started walking back the way she came. Milly thought about protesting, but she knew it was unlikely that she would be able to change her friend's mind.

The girls had been using a long pole for the past few days to feed the skunk. At first it threatened to spray in their direction every time the pole got near it, but after a while it started to recognize that it represented an opportunity to get food.

They had even started to hook the pole through the handle of the cage, lift it a few feet off the ground, and swing it around when they fed the creature to get it used to the motion. Now that Sarah was walking back up the dirt road, Milly knew that she had decided it was worth the risk to try and incorporate the animal for their plan after all.

Once they reached the caged skunk and the pole, Sarah ran to her sack and pulled out an apple. She used her pocket knife to cut it up into several small pieces. She pulled out a ball of twine and used it to tie the apple slices to the pole.

She told Milly to stand behind her, and she worked the long stick of wood into the handle of the cage. The skunk immediately started reaching through the top of the cage, clawing for the treats. Sarah hooked the pole under her arm for leverage and lifted up the cage. She walked as fast as she could while carrying the awkward load. The wild beast didn't seem to be paying any attention to the two girls as it continued to pull down pieces of the apple.

It took them nearly twenty minutes to make it back to the other cages. Sarah whispered for Milly to grab one of the cages and follow her down the hill. They moved slowly down the hill until they were about fifty feet away from the cabin. After setting the cages down, they crouched down behind a bush and looked into a large window of the structure.

All the lights were off, but they could see into the main living area. Sarah moved in closer, grabbed onto the windowsill, and pulled herself up to get a better view. She could see that two young men were sleeping in the area. One was lying on the couch and another one was sleeping in a large chair. She recognized them both as part of Claud Stimpson's crew. She turned back and told Milly what she had seen.

Sarah was certain that the cabin belonged to Claud, and she snuck around to the front and saw his rusty old truck parked out front. The cabin had at least two bedrooms, and she was now certain that he was sleeping in one of them.

Satisfied that they had enough of the bullies

together to set their trap, they walked around to the back of the cabin. The back door was wide open, with only a flimsy screen door covering the entryway to keep out the flies.

The girls moved the cages around to the back and set them down just outside the door. Then they went back up the hill to grab the two remaining cages with the raccoons.

Sarah opened the screen door slowly, trying hard not to let it creak too loudly. She used a log from the woodpile to prop it open. They knew the skunk was going to be the trickiest animal to deal with, so they started with it first. Milly used the pole to pick up the smelly creature, and it immediately started grabbing at the remaining pieces of fruit. Once the cage was at the door, Sarah moved to the back of the cage and opened the back of the trap. The animal was now free to leave. Milly walked forward and sat the cage down deep inside the cabin. She continued holding onto the pole, as the skunk stayed focused on eating.

Sarah quickly moved the opossum inside the back porch and opened the trap. The lazy animal just stayed in place acting like it was sleeping or dead. She grabbed the two raccoons and put them in place. She loosened the latches and looked back at Milly, making sure she was ready. Her friend nodded, and Sarah turned around and lifted the cage doors. The raccoons dashed out in a hurry, running into the cabin.

Sarah scurried backward running into Milly who dropped the pole. The sudden rattling of the cage startled the skunk and it raised and pointed its hind end up in the air. The girls froze in place. After a few agonizing seconds, the beast went back to eating a hunk of fruit it had in its paws.

Sarah kicked the log away from the screen door and it screeched loudly as it slammed shut. She could only imagine how the skunk and other animals would react to the noise. The girls didn't wait around to find out. Instead, they started running up the hill has fast as their legs would carry them. Milly even forgot about her wounded leg in the moment and was running hard while carrying her crutch.

Once they reached the top of the hill, they found a place to hide that still had a decent view of the house. They waited for the fireworks to start.

Cabin of Chaos

It didn't take long for the commotion to start in the cabin. One of the bullies let out a loud yelp, which was followed by a crashing noise. From the sound of the yelling, the raccoons had reached the living room.

A second scream came from somewhere in the cabin. It wasn't certain where the occupant was located, but they were clearly complaining about the opossum. A few more banging and crashing sounds rang out.

The girls burst into laughter at all the wonderful noises. They moved down the hill to get a better look, hiding behind a large tree. They moved even further to the side to get a look at the front door. A few minutes later, they saw one of the bullies run out the door followed by a raccoon. The boy turned around after jumping off the porch. He bent over holding onto his arm, trying to catch his breath.

A few seconds later someone in the house yelled, "Skunk!" It was more of a high-pitched squeal than a shout. The girls laughed even harder when they heard that the smelly animal had been spotted.

The man standing outside the cabin stood up sharply and rushed back in through the door. This seemed odd to Sarah. Why would anyone want to run back into a house with all those wild beasts running around, especially an awful skunk?

The crashing and banging increased and there was cacophony of yelling and shouting. Suddenly the noises stopped for a moment, and the second raccoon came running out.

Sarah couldn't believe that the bullies had not come out of the house yet. The spotting of a skunk should have immediately cleared the room. She started to get a sinking feeling and decided to move in a bit closer. Milly followed behind her, as they shuffled further to the side in order to get a full view of the front of the cabin.

They hadn't heard any new noises in about a minute. Sarah looked over at Milly, who was no longer smiling. It was clear that she was also sensing that something was amiss.

That's when they heard a second high-pitched scream followed by, "There's a skunk in my room!" The sound did not come from a boy. It was the voice of a girl, and most likely someone young; even younger than Sarah and Milly.

The girls looked at each other with wide eyes. They hadn't seen a woman in the room, and certainly no children. But they hadn't been able to see into the bedrooms. They never considered that there might be girls in the cabin. Claud was barely out of high school, and he wasn't known to have a girlfriend. The only people Sarah had ever seen with him were his bully friends.

More yelling caught the girls' attention, and the opossum could be seen tumbling out the front door, followed by one of the boys carrying a broom. He swatted the opossum on the rear end, launching it off the porch. The boy turned around and ran back inside the house.

Milly grabbed onto Sarah's arm and pulled her in closer. She was shaking. There wasn't anything the girls could do but watch and listen.

A few seconds later, even louder banging could be heard, followed by a chorus of yelling from both boys and girls. Then there was a loud crash. "I've got it! Get out of the way!"

Claud came running out of the front door carrying the wild beast. Unfortunately, he was holding the skunk in the wrong direction and took a blast directly in the face from the frightened animal. The stream of liquid must have blinded him, and he stumbled forward. Still holding onto the critter, he tumbled down the steps of the porch and crashed hard to the ground. He screamed out in pain as he tossed the skunk away from him and grabbed his leg. Another bully ran to help him up. Claud cried out in pain as his friend tried to stand him up. He pushed him away and dropped him back to the ground still holding on to his leg.

The skunk was crouching about ten feet away from the two boys and was startled by the loud yelling. It reared up on its haunches and coated both bullies with another stream of smelly liquid. Then the beast ran off toward the river.

Claud let go of his leg and used his arm to block some of the spray. The second boy fell backwards onto the porch and grabbed at his chest. He pulled off his flannel shirt and tossed it to the side, trying to get away from the horrible smell.

On the hillside, the girls watched the scene unfold. Their eyes had started to water as the smell from the skunk had reached their position. They were both anxious to get out of the area, but they had to stick around to see what happened next. They also needed to see who else had been in the cabin.

Two more boys came out of the cabin holding their noses. They helped lift their friend up from the porch then gathered around Claud. Someone handed him a rag, and he began wiping the skunk spray off his face. It was obvious that he was still blinded by the oily substance. "Where's my sister? Where's Becky and the baby?"

"They are safe inside. I am pretty sure we got everything out of the cabin. Now, what the hell is going on?"

"Hell if I know, but get your asses back in there and make sure there isn't anything else crawling around."

"Alright, Claud. But then we got to get you over to Doc Goldman to get that leg checked out. It looks broken."

Two of the guys went back inside the house, while the boy on the porch grabbed a bucket and ran down to the river to fetch some water. A woman appeared in the doorway holding a young girl in her arms.

Sarah heard Milly whimper at the sight of the child. The little girl couldn't be more than three or four years old, and she looked scared to death. Even from a distance, they could see that tears were streaming down her face, and they could tell that her lips were quivering.

Sarah now had tears in her eyes. She couldn't tell if it was because of the smell or the sight of the pitiful little girl who was holding her tiny nose. She looked over at Milly who also had tears in her eyes.

They watched as the boys loaded Claud into the back of the pickup. One got into the cab and started the engine, while the one who had been sprayed got in the back to help Claud.

"Travis, get Becky and my niece back in the house. Then use the hose to clean off all this nasty stuff and for the love of Saint Pete, figure out what the hell is going on."

Travis nodded and turned toward the girls. He led them back inside and closed the door.

Sarah and Milly had to lay down flat on the

ground as the pickup climbed the hill and drove down the dirt road passing ten feet in front of them. Once it was out of sight, they jumped up and headed down the road. They walked in silence trying to process everything they had seen.

Sarah was thankful for the silence and the fact that Milly was walking slightly behind her. The wind was cold on her face as a stream of tears flowed down her cheeks.

Bitter Victory

The moon was still high in the sky as the girls arrived at the clearing where they had staged their supplies. Sarah pulled her gunny sack out from behind a bush and took out the blanket. They leaned against the log again and huddled beneath the blanket.

Sarah felt a wave of sadness as she looked down at the brightly colored quilt. It had been hand made by her grandmother. It was the last Christmas gift she had received from the wonderful lady, and now it had been used as part of this horrible caper.

She reached into the sack and pulled out the canteen. After taking a swig, she handed it to Milly who took a drink. The girls hadn't said a word in nearly thirty minutes.

After a while longer, Sarah reached into her sack and pulled out the two Baby Ruth candy bars. She handed one to Milly who looked up at her. "Do we really deserve these?"

"Probably not, but we're going to eat them anyway."

Milly looked down at the red lettering on the package but didn't open it. She looked like she was searching for the right thing to say.

"I know, Milly. We didn't mean to scare that child or her mother. We wouldn't have gone through with the plan if we had known they were in there. There isn't anything we can do about that now."

Milly looked up at her with watery eyes. She still didn't know what to say.

"We may not be able to eat these as a victory celebration, but I think we should eat them just the same."

"But why, Sarah? I just feel awful right now. We were supposed to punish those bullies, not become bullies ourselves."

"I know. I feel awful, too. But we said we were going to eat this candy when we were done, and I think we should follow through with it. I know it doesn't make sense." She looked down at the package. "My daddy always says that no matter how hard life gets, you can always eat a Baby Ruth."

Milly looked up at her confused and flashed a bit of anger. "Your daddy never said such a foolish thing in all his life."

Sarah looked at her friend for a second, then bowed her head. Tears started to fall from her eyes. "I know, but I don't know what else to do. I just feel so bad about all this."

It broke Milly's heart to see Sarah cry. She was the strongest person she knew. In all the times they had been together, she had never seen her cry. Even when she broke her arm last year tumbling down a hill, she never saw her shed a single tear.

"Well, he may not have said it, but I think it is a right good idea. If we can't have a victory candy bar, then we can at least have a candy bar as friends. Besides, that little girl will remember tonight for the rest of her life. When she's our age she will probably laugh about it."

Milly stiffened up her lip and tore open the Baby Ruth and took a big bite. She looked silly chewing on the large wad of candy, and Sarah couldn't keep herself from laughing.

The girls snuggled up together under the blanket and ate their candy together. When they were finished, they pulled the blanket up tighter. Sarah looked over at Milly who had chocolate on the corners of her mouth.

"I will never forget the look on Claud's face as he came running out of the house with that skunk," she said as she looked up at the stars.

Milly looked at Sarah and smiled. "And the look of terror on that shirtless boy's face as he tried to wipe away the horrible smell."

The girls continued reliving the incident throughout the rest of the night. They still felt bad about the frightened little girl, but the guilt subsided a bit with each bite.

Home Sweet Home

The bright sun shining through the trees woke the girls up the next morning. They were still warm under the blanket, but it was now damp with dew. They were reluctant to slip out of their warm cocoon, but they had to get going in order to get back to Sarah's house before anyone started looking for them.

Sarah folded up the quilt and stuffed it into her sack, along with the canteen and candy bar wrappers. They walked out of the clearing and found the bike still hidden in the brush.

They got on the bike and headed back up the dirt road and turned onto the main gravel road toward Sarah's house. They could see that a vehicle was heading their way. Sarah's heart started pounding when she saw that it was Claud's rusty old truck. She pulled over to the side of the road and stopped. Leaning back, she told Milly what was going on, and they both turned to look at the approaching vehicle.

They thought about ducking into the woods, but there wasn't enough time. Instead, they just stayed on the side of the road and watched the truck draw closer. The driver slowed down as it passed the girls, and they could see inside. Claud was sitting up in the back of the truck with his leg propped up on a crate. His leg was covered in a large white cast that went all the way up to his hip. It was nearly identical to the one Milly had to wear when she first broke her leg.

The boys in the back of the truck barely noticed the

girls standing by the side of the road. They just sat quietly in the truck staring off into the horizon. Once the truck passed out of sight, Sarah looked over at Milly with her mouth wide in amazement. Milly just shrugged her shoulders. "I guess the Good Lord decided there should be a leg for a leg this time."

Sarah wasn't sure what to think about her friend's harsh comment. It wasn't like Milly to be so cold. All she could do was smile and shake her head.

They jumped back on the bike and finished the ride to Sarah' house. Sarah's brother Victor met them at the front door as they approached. He was carrying a basket of apples and looked unhappy to be working on chores on such a warm, sunny morning.

Sarah's mother followed him out of the house carrying the apple peeler and a large pot.

"You girls got here just in time. We were about to start making some apple butter."

Sarah grabbed the apple peeler from her mother and handed it to Milly. Then she grabbed the basket from her brother. "We'll peel the apples, Momma. Victor can go play, and you can sit in the house. We'll bring them in when we're done and start cooking them up."

Sarah's mother wasn't sure how to react to her daughter's sudden willingness to do chores. Before she could say anything, Sarah and Milly were already heading to the outdoor table to start working on the apples. She put her hands on her hips and watched them as they walked away. Victor wasted no time in making his escape, as he rushed off to find his bike.

Sarah knew that her actions were suspicious. She was not known to volunteer for housework or cooking. She would jump at the chance to work with her dad at the woodworking shop or to go out on the farm, but she hated domestic chores.

None of that mattered now. The girls were just happy to have something to do for the day. They needed to make amends for scaring that little girl; for becoming bullies. Making apple butter wasn't much of a penance, but it was at least a start.

It took them nearly two hours to peel, slice, and wash all the apples. They tossed the fruit into a large stock pot and headed into the kitchen. They added in a whole sack of white sugar and a carton of brown sugar and started stirring the mixture. Sarah lit the flame and continued stirring, as Milly added in some cinnamon, nutmeg, and cloves.

The house was filled with a wonderful smell when Sarah's mother came back inside carrying an armful of zucchini. She inspected the pot and determined that the mixture met her satisfaction. Sarah grabbed the vegetables from her mother and set them on the counter. She told Milly to get out the flour and they started gathering all the ingredients to make zucchini bread.

Her mother looked curiously at the girls. Something strange was definitely going on in their little heads, but she wasn't going to stop them from doing chores. Instead, she sat down on her rocking chair and started knitting on a scarf.

It was late afternoon when the girls finished the

apple butter and zucchini bread. They had even cooked up a batch of fried chicken and okra for dinner.

Elwood came home just after dark and sat down at the dinner table. Sarah brought him a plate of food and sat down beside Milly on the couch. He looked at the girls, who were covered head to toe in flour and other ingredients. He looked over at Momma, who just shrugged her shoulders.

"You girls look like you worked hard today."

"We just thought we should help out around the house. We got to play all day yesterday, so it was only fair that we take a turn doing the chores."

Elwood wasn't totally convinced by the magnanimous gesture, but he did like having fried chicken for dinner. By the time he was finished, both Sarah and Milly were fast asleep. He tossed a cover over them and sat down in his rocking chair beside Momma.

He wasn't sure what was going on with the girls, but he figured it would all work out eventually. Sarah was never very good at keeping secrets, and something was obviously gnawing at her insides. That is the only thing that could explain why she would volunteer to do work inside the house.

Father Daughter Time

Milly ran out to meet her mother as she pulled up in the car the next morning. She couldn't risk her getting out and talking to Sarah's mom about her trip to Louisville. She jumped in the car just as it stopped moving.

Milly's mom waved as they turned around in the driveway. Milly could be seen in the back window waving as they pulled away.

Sarah pulled on her overalls and laced up her thick leather boots. Her father had asked her to go with him to the workshop after breakfast to help sort through bundles of wood staves that would eventually be used to make oak barrels. She didn't particularly like working with wood, but she was always happy to be invited to the workshop.

With any luck, she might be able to convince her father to let her fire up the forge and bend some of the pieces of iron into hoops. She loved working with metal, and she knew that her father had recently purchased a new anvil with an extended horn that would make it much easier to bend the hoops.

Momma scolded her a few times for eating too quickly, but finally told her to get up from the table and get her things ready. Sarah ran to her room and grabbed her gunny sack. She threw in her baseball cap, a pair of heavy gloves, and an extra t-shirt in case she got dirty.

She was waiting on the porch when Elwood came outside carrying his heavy green thermos. The man was known to drink coffee from sun up to sun down most every day of the week. He waved for Sarah to head to the truck, and they started the short drive to the workshop.

Sarah rolled the window down and let her hand glide in the breeze during the ten minute drive to the south end of the farm. She jumped out as they arrived at the workshop and opened the large double doors so that her father could back the truck into the shop. They both unloaded the staves, and her father used a pair of cutters to snap the band holding them together.

Sarah ran back and forth sorting out the staves. Each stick of wood first needed to be inspected for straightness and quality. Any that had knots or other imperfections had to be thrown in the discard pile. The pieces that passed inspection were sorted by size and placed in large boxes.

Elwood chuckled to himself as he watched his daughter move with lightning speed sorting through the staves. He knew she was trying to buy extra time in the forge. After nearly an hour all the wood had been sorted, and Sarah grabbed a broom and swept the area clean. She threw away the debris, hung the broom on a hook, and looked at her father pleadingly.

Elwood stood quietly looking over a clipboard pretending not to notice her. She softly cleared her throat to get his attention. Finally, he looked up over his reading glasses. "I suppose you want to fire up the forge don't you?"

"I just thought I would help make a few hoops if you wanted me to."

"Go ahead and fire up the large one in the front." He hadn't finished his sentence and she was already in motion. "Just be careful now. Your momma will tan both our hides if you burn yourself."

Sarah put on a leather apron then dumped a pile of coal into the forge and started turning the blower to make sure the air was flowing properly. She lit a torch and started heating the coal pieces while cranking the blower as fast as her skinny arms would move. In a matter of minutes, she had the center of the pile glowing red hot.

She placed a few skinny bars of metal on the edges of the fire and let them heat up. She slipped on her gloves, grabbed a pair of tongs, and picked up a two pound sledge hammer. She started hammering the thin metal strips into perfectly round hoops.

Elwood continued walking around the workshop and writing in his clipboard and sipping coffee. He looked up every once in a while to check on his daughter. He had always been amazed at how quickly she could bend steel. Even with her skinny frame and small hammer, she could move metal faster and with more precision than many of his seasoned workers.

After two hours, Sarah had created hoops out of all the cut metal pieces. She was covered in a mix of sweat and coal dust, but she was still smiling from ear to ear. Elwood told her to go into the office and clean herself up.

When she was ready, they headed into town to order extra metal sheets and pick up some rivets before heading to the local diner to grab lunch. They sat down and ordered hamburgers, fries, and chocolate milkshakes. Sarah couldn't believe her luck.

First, she got to work the forge and now she was getting a milkshake.

Once the orders were in, her father sat back in his chair and looked at a newspaper he had picked up from the bin. He waited a few minutes before speaking. "You know I heard through that rumor mill that young Claud Stimpson broke his leg last night."

"Mmm. Hmm." Sarah mumbled as she picked up the menu and pretended to read it.

"It turns out his house was vandalized by some hooligans who let a bunch critters loose in there."

"I see. Critters you say."

"Yes, and one of those critters was a smelly old skunk like the one you and Milly came across."

Sarah continued to bow her head and let her hair fall down in front of her face. She knew she was in trouble now, but she was trying to hide her face anyway.

Elwood folded up the paper and laid in on the table. "I know those boys have been bullying you for a while now. I suspect they might have had something to do with Milly getting hurt."

He paused for a while waiting for a response.

"Yes, Daddy."

He did his best to hide his grin. "You know your momma wouldn't approve of such a thing. She would say that's just not how good Christian folks behave."

"Yes, Daddy."

He picked up his paper and started reading it again. "I'm sure your momma will have more to say about it all when you get home. That rumor mill works pretty fast in these parts."

"Yes, Daddy."

"But, I suppose spending three hours busting your hump in the forge today should be punishment enough. You were just standing up for your friend and all. The Good Lord did say to turn the other cheek, but I suppose he never did say anything about skunks."

Sarah let a little giggle escape as she wiped a tear from her eye. She thought about saying more, but the waitress interrupted the conversation with a tray of food.

They started eating and Sarah looked up at her father. He smiled at her and gave her a wink. She could take all the scolding her mother had to offer, as long as she knew that she hadn't disappointed her daddy.

CANCER – PART 3

"Somedays life is all about your dreams, hopes, and visions for the future. But there are somedays where life is just about putting one foot in front of the other. And that's okay."

– Author Unknown

The Surgery

Sarah sat on the bench seat looking out the window of the recovery room. She wished she was at home in her own bedroom looking out at her backyard. That had been the plan anyway, but now she was going on day four in the hospital.

The double mastectomy had hit a snag. They had removed both of her breasts as planned but they also learned that the cancer had spread into the lymph nodes in her left armpit more aggressively than first believed. This meant that they had to cut through some muscle and other vital pieces of tissue to reach the tumors.

The first three days of recovery were the hardest, and she could barely move without feeling like she was tearing the muscles on her left side. She also had to lay and sleep on her right side, which had begun to cramp up. Plus, it made going to the bathroom extremely difficult.

To make matters worse, she hadn't been allowed any visitors due to her extensive open wounds. She had no doubt that Lucas would be worried sick at the change in plans, and she knew he was probably berating the doctors about not being able to see to her.

By the end of the third day, the nurse took the catheter out and she was allowed to use the restroom on her own. They also changed the dressings on her chest, arms, and shoulder, which were now tighter and allowed her to lay on her back without disturbing the muscles on her left side nearly as much.

Lucas was also allowed to visit her that evening. He looked as exhausted as she felt when he entered the room. Thankfully, he was allowed to stay with her that night, and he slept in the recliner beside her bed. He managed to sleep through the night, even as the nurses came in and out of the room every couple hours.

Now it was day four and Sarah was finally able to move freely around the room. She continued staring out the window at the hospital courtyard. She looked over at Lucas, who was still sleeping in the chair. It was nearly nine o'clock in the morning.

She couldn't remember the last time her husband had slept in that late. She chuckled to herself as she looked at his tall slim frame tucked into the small lounge chair. His feet hung over the ends of the footrest and his head poked over the top of the chair. Somehow, he still managed a deep enough sleep to induce a soft snoring sound.

The surgeon walked into the room a few minutes later causing Lucas to jump to his feet. He wiped the sleep from his eyes and folded away the blanket as Sarah walked back to the bed. The surgeon asked the nurse to unwrap the dressings around Sarah's chest and shoulder so that he could inspect the wounds.

Sarah stared blankly out the window as it all happened. Her modesty had taken several hits over the past few months nearly a dozen doctors and nurses had now seen her without her shirt on. No matter how many times she had to get undressed for medical reasons, she still felt embarrassed by the process.

Now that she was disfigured by the surgery, she was even more embarrassed. Everyone was always so kind in their responses, but that did little to ease her mind. She would always do her best to avoid eye contact, as much for the benefit of others as her own bashfulness.

Once the bandages had been removed, the surgeon quickly surveyed the damage. He waved Lucas over and described what had been done during the procedure.

Sarah and Lucas had both watched videos online of the surgery, so they had an idea of what to expect. However, the extent of the tissue removal was much more severe in Sarah's case.

Her cancer was more aggressive, and the surgeon had to completely remove both breasts, including the nipples, areolas, and much of the skin. This would make the reconstruction process much more extensive if that was even an option in the future.

The incisions around Sarah's armpit were the most shocking. This part of the operation had not been expected, and the cuts were long and looked very deep in some places. Sarah's arm would need to remain in a sling for a few weeks in order to keep the incisions from opening up.

The surgeon showed Lucas how to apply the ointments and wrap the bandages over the wounded areas. He continually stressed the importance of resting over the next month. It was going to take a while for Sarah to heal, and she would need all the strength she could muster to handle the aggressive radiation and chemotherapy sessions that awaited her.

After the surgeon left, Lucas called the rest of the family to give them an update. He was careful not to lie to his sons, but he also didn't tell them everything that had been done during the surgery.

They wouldn't be able to leave the hospital until the next morning, and the boys said they would be waiting outside as soon as their mother was released.

The rest of the day went by slowly as more nurses and doctors visited to set follow up appointments and deliver more instructions. When it was time for bed, the nurse came in and unhooked the IV. She told them that she would do her best not to disturb them until morning. This was a relief to Sarah. She hadn't gone more than a couple hours without a stranger walking into her room in the past four days, and she desperately wanted some time alone with just her and Lucas.

She laid down on the bed and rolled over on her side so that she could look out the window. She began to cry. She wasn't sad or in pain. She couldn't really say why the tears were coming, but she needed to cry just the same.

She felt Lucas slip under the covers and move in beside her on the small bed. He wrapped his arms around her as gently as he could. He kissed her on the neck and laid his head next to hers. He didn't say a word, which was perfect.

She didn't need him to say anything or do anything. She just needed him to be there with her in that moment.

BOOTLEG ROMANCE

"Whiskey, like a beautiful woman, demands appreciation. You gaze first, then it's time to drink."

– Haruki Murakami

Winter 1962

A Welcome Stranger

Sarah Blackstone pulled her shoulder length black hair into a ponytail and tied on her heavy leather blacksmithing apron. She started the fire on the forge and set it on the lowest heat setting. She then placed a heavy iron plate on top of the rack and let it heat up for a few minutes.

She had to make sure that the plate didn't get too hot; otherwise, the galvanized steel bands would emit a poisonous gas that would damage her lungs when breathed in. She put a thermometer on the iron plate and saw that the temperature was holding steady at 350 degrees.

She only needed to soften the metal just enough to allow her to easily hammer it into round hoops that could be fastened around the oak barrels. Now that the iron plate was ready, she placed a bundle of two-inch-wide flat pieces of galvanized steel on the plate and let them warm to the proper temperature.

She slipped on her heavy blacksmithing gloves, grabbed a pair of large tongs, and lifted a narrow piece of steel over to the anvil. She picked up her three-pound sledgehammer and started working the metal on the horn of the anvil until it formed a circle. She looked over the hoop to make sure it passed her inspection, then tossed it into the bin.

Sarah and her brother Victor had decided to close the Blackstone Oak Barrel Company for the two weeks surrounding Christmas and New Year's Day. They had been running hard for the past year, now that they had become the largest oak barrel maker in the region. The employees needed a break, and so did they.

Victor had decided to head south for his time off to visit the panhandle of Florida. He had never seen the ocean, and this was his first real vacation since becoming an adult.

Sarah stayed in town to catch up on paperwork and watch over the shop. During normal operations, she spent her time working in the office handling the day-to-day business of the company, but she missed working with metal in the shop.

With the workshop empty, she took the opportunity to bend some hoops. She spent the morning and most of the afternoon working the steel, and she was now covered in sweat, dirt, and black coal dust. She had completed two bins worth of hoops and was finishing up her last band when a tall, thin man appeared in the doorway of the workshop. He looked like a vision as the sun backlit him creating a silhouette. She could tell that he was wearing a military uniform and carrying a seabag. She let the hammer hang down to her side as she smiled at him.

"You told me to stop by Kentucky if I ever had some spare time," said the Marine as he removed the seabag from his shoulder. "So, this is what you look like in your natural environment."

Sarah could not believe that Lucas Fosterman was standing in her workshop. She had been writing to the young Marine for several months. They had swapped dozens of stories about their adventures over the past year.

She had shared with him about her father's death and her family's fight to keep the Blackstone Oak Barrel Company in business. She had been more honest in those letters than she had been with anyone before.

Lucas had also shared stories of his time serving at a small air station in Japan. He had written about his daily adventures with men that had strange nicknames like Tadpole, Archie, Kilgore, and Bruno.

They had both written about their families and shared their feelings about love and loss. Even though she had only briefly met the man in a hotel bar in Tacoma just over a year ago during a business trip, she still felt a strong connection to him. They had only gotten to spend a few fun days together before she had to leave abruptly after her father's second heart attack.

She had always hoped she would see him again, but she never imagined he would show up one day out of the blue. Now here he was in Kentucky, standing in front of her.

Sarah shut off the forge and removed her gloves. She tossed the hammer onto the table and grabbed a rag to wipe the sweat and black soot off her brow. She must have looked quite the sight with her dirty face and sweat-soaked shirt.

Lucas didn't care about any of that as he walked in closer to her. He hesitated for a second but decided he had come too far to chicken out now. He moved in close and embraced her. They shared a long kiss before sitting down to catch up.

They sat quietly at first, not knowing how to start the emotionally-charged conversation. Lucas had plenty to tell her about, since he needed to explain the recent events that had led to his arrival.

Less than three days ago, he had been in Japan attending his friend Bruno's funeral service after the man committed suicide. He had taken his life after receiving a "Dear John" letter and could not take the heartache and isolation that so many Marines felt being separated from home on the small island country. Someone had to bring Bruno's body back to his mother in Tennessee, and since Lucas was the next man scheduled to rotate out, he was assigned the task.

In the course of less than seventy-two hours he had lost a friend, been promoted, received new orders to California, and flown back to the states. Now he was sitting in a workshop in Kentucky with the most beautiful woman he had ever known.

Lucas had more than a month of leave saved up, and he was not due to arrive at the USS *Midway* until mid-February. He wasn't sure what he was going to do with his time off, but he knew it involved Sarah and staying with her for as long as she would have him. He had plenty of money saved up, so he planned to rent a room for the next couple weeks and take things from there.

They talked late into the afternoon before Sarah drove Lucas into town. Bloomfield was a very small town located less than an hour away from both Louisville to the north and Lexington to the west. It was the closest town to the Blackstone Workshop, and it only contained a few small businesses. Luckily, there was a room available at the small-town inn.

Lucas checked into the hotel and stowed away his gear before meeting Sarah across the street at the diner. The town also had a decent size general store, which Lucas planned to visit when it opened the next morning to purchase some new clothes.

After dinner, Sarah hugged Lucas goodbye and told him she would meet him the next morning for breakfast at the diner at nine. They planned to spend the day together, and she promised to show him around the area.

Bourbon Country

The next morning Lucas rose early and headed to the general store. He purchased a couple pair of blue jeans, a few shirts, and some boots before heading back to the hotel to swap clothes. He was glad to be out of his uniform for a change.

He had worn the same class "B" service uniform nearly every day for the past year. He folded up his green trousers, khaki shirt, and tie and stuffed them into his seabag. He then wrapped his polished black shoes in a white t-shirt and stuffed then into the bag as well. He didn't plan to wear the uniform again until he reported for duty.

He tossed on some jeans and a flannel shirt and looked at himself in the mirror. His short, cropped hair still gave away his occupation, but at least he didn't stand out so much as he did when wearing his uniform. He stored away his seabag in the closet and headed out to the diner.

He was already sitting at a booth drinking coffee when Sarah walked in. She looked beautiful in a pretty yellow sun dress.

"Well, you look pretty today."

"It helps that I'm not covered in coal and wearing a big leather apron. You look almost human wearing normal clothes."

"Are you saying I don't look human in uniform?"

"You just looked so official and all. Plus, you always stand straight as an arrow."

Lucas laughed at the thought. He had always been overly proper when in uniform. He just didn't know how awkward it must look to civilians. "I will do my best to act more human over the next few days."

"Well thank you, I would appreciate that."

The two had a good laugh and ordered breakfast. After eating, they jumped in Sarah's green International pickup and headed out for a tour of the countryside.

During the drive Sarah told Lucas all about Kentucky's bourbon country, which mainly included the areas immediately outside of Louisville and

Lexington with a few pockets of land in between. She also described to him the differences between whiskey and bourbon.

Lucas was fascinated by the process, and he could see that Sarah received great enjoyment in talking about all things related to making whiskey.

She explained that whiskey was a made from fermented grain called a mash that was aged in barrels. Rot-gut whiskey, as she called it, could be aged in any old barrels; including ones used to age wine, rum, or some other liquor.

To be called bourbon, whiskey had to be distilled from a mash that was at least 51 percent corn. That mash must then be aged in new charred oak barrels. The aging process for bourbon normally lasted a minimum of two years, which allowed distillers to call their liquor "straight bourbon whiskey." However, the truly respectable distillers aged their liquor at least four years and had special batches that were eight, ten, and even fifteen years old.

Sarah went on for hours describing the distillation process and went into even greater detail about barrel making and what made for a quality barrel that was fit to age premium bourbon. Lucas enjoyed every second of the lesson, and only interrupted a few times to ask questions.

It wasn't until the afternoon that Sarah realized that she had been droning on about nothing but liquor and her homeland all day. The realization made her blush a little. She had never been a big talker, and she couldn't believe that she had monopolized over four hours of conversation.

"Well, that is probably more than you ever wanted to know about whiskey."

"No. It is fascinating. Really, I enjoyed the advanced lesson. I will certainly never confuse plain old whiskey with bourbon again that's for sure. I wouldn't want to offend my teacher."

Sarah punched him in the arm and scowled at him. "Well then, tell me more about Japan."

"There isn't much more to tell than I what I wrote to you about in my letters. We weren't let outside the base much, so my version of Japan was just sitting on a large rock in the ocean drinking way too much beer. The guys I served with were the only real interesting part of the island. You know all about Tadpole, Archie, Kilgore, and of course poor Bruno."

"That was really sad about Bruno. I can't believe he would hang himself over a girl."

"It's amazing what a man will do for a girl. I mean look at me. I flew halfway around the world just to get a lesson on the finer points of whiskey from a pretty girl."

Sarah blushed again and turned her head to look out the window so that Lucas couldn't see her grin. She was enjoying her time with the young Marine.

More Whiskey

Sarah knocked on Lucas' door at eight the next morning. She told him yesterday that his lesson on making proper whiskey wouldn't be complete without a tour of a distillery, and she was ready to make good on that promise.

Lucas opened the door and told her to come in. He was wearing his jeans but hadn't yet put on his t-shirt or a flannel. He turned his back to her as he grabbed a white t-shirt off the back of a chair and slipped it on. Since his back was to her, Sarah took the opportunity to peak at his naked torso. Lucas was a bit too thin, but he had a muscular back and broad shoulders. She watched as he pulled the shirt down and averted her eyes before he turned back around.

Sarah caught her reflection in the mirror and noticed that she was blushing. Lucas asked her to grab him a flannel shirt out of his closet, and she picked a blue one to match the color of his eyes.

Instead of the old green International, Sarah was driving the Ford stake bed truck today. She had a small load of fifteen barrels in the back, which she needed to drop off at the Bowman Distillery. The two jumped into the pickup and drove about thirty minutes toward Louisville before turning off at the large distillery located a few blocks off the highway.

Marty Bowman was standing outside of his main building watching two of his employees load boxes of liquor into a Chevy panel truck that was marked up with the company's logos. Sarah backed the truck up to the large double doors leading into the building and jumped out.

"Good morning, Mister Bowman. How are you doing today?"

"For Pete's sake Sarah, am I ever going to get you to call my Marty? You've known me since you were knee high to a grasshopper. "

"No, sir. If you my daddy didn't call you Marty, then I don't reckon it would be right for me to either."

"Very well. Who's this you got with you. I thought you gave all your workers the week off?"

"I did, Mister Bowman. This is Lucas. He's a friend of mine. He's a Marine on leave for a spell."

"I see, and he decided to spend his hard-earned vacation here in backwoods Kentucky for some strange reason?" Marty shot her a suspicious grin as he walked by her to shake Lucas' hand.

"Any friend of Sarah Backstone is surely a friend of mine." He whistled for one of the men loading the truck to come over.

"Hey Tim, grab the keys from Sarah and unload the barrels off her truck. Make sure to keep these barrels separate from the others. They should be stacked in the back by the rye mash."

Sarah handed him the keys and he ran off to open the double doors. "Mister Bowman, I was hoping to get Lucas a tour of the distillery. I have been bending his ear for the past few days about the process, and it would be nice to show him what it looks like in real life."

"Well come on in, I would be happy to show you around. We don't have much brewing because of the holiday and all, but he should be able to get a good idea of how it all works."

Over the next hour, the excited owner walked

Lucas around every corner of his business. He showed him around all the large wood vats, steel boilers, and copper stills. By the end of the tour Lucas' head was swimming with new terms like thumper, head, mash, bubblers, tailings, and worms. And he really couldn't understand what a raccoon penis had to do with making liquor. Mister Bowman had mentioned the "coon dick" hanging from the spigot of some of the stills to direct the final product into glass jugs.

The tour had helped provide a visual reference for many of the descriptions Sarah had provided him. However, he still had a long way to go before he would truly understand the full process.

At the end of the tour, they arrived at a large copper still surrounded by the fifteen barrels that the men had unloaded from Sarah's truck. Lucas looked at the barrels and noticed that they were less charred inside than most of the other barrels he had seen in the building. He could also tell that the smell coming from the copper vat wasn't as sweet as the others he had been around.

"This process seems different than everything else I've seen today."

Mister Bowman smiled and walked over and slapped the copper still. "That is correct. This mash is not going to be bourbon. This is for a batch of rye whiskey."

He went on to explain that rye whiskey was unique because it was made with at least fifty one percent rye. For his recipe, he liked to lighten the charring in the barrels and aged it for a minimum of five years before bottling it.

As Lucas listened to the man describe the liquor he could tell that he took great pride in his rye whiskey. "I thought bourbon was what put Kentucky on the map."

"That's true, and it has made me a lot of money over the years. But there is more to this tradition than labels. You see whiskey is a drink, bourbon is an identity, but rye whiskey is a legacy. Anyone can make whiskey, but bourbon takes a special hand to perfect. When it comes to rye, well, really good rye whiskey is what separates the good distilleries from the legendary ones."

"Then you must have a great rye whiskey."

"I work on my recipe every year, but I still have a ways to go. If you really want to try something special, you'll have to see if Sarah will give you a sip of her father Elwood's rye. He made the best I have ever tasted."

Lucas looked to the back of the building and spotted Sarah with a clipboard counting up stacks of barrels and making notations. He must have stared at her for longer than he realized because Mister Bowman walked up next to him and looked across the way.

"I must say, I have known Sarah since she was a seedling. In all her years, she has never brought a friend to visit my distillery. If you can keep her as a friend, then you are about the luckiest young man in all of Kentucky."

Lucas nodded subconsciously. He was still getting to know Sarah, but he had little doubt that Mister Bowman was correct. He wasn't going to find a woman like her again, so he better make his time with her count.

Calling in a Favor

After the visit to the distillery, Sarah and Lucas drove back into town to eat at the diner. Lucas was talking excitedly about everything he had learned during the tour, and Sarah was pleased to see that he was enjoying his time in bourbon country. She had worried that she had overdone it with all the talk about whiskey.

They had just ordered pie for dessert when the bell on the diner door rang. Sarah looked over to see Old Man Cinder walk in with a serious look on his face. He scanned the booths quickly, then spotted her sitting in the corner. He approached the table taking off his hat as he moved in closer.

"Good evening, Sarah, sorry to bother you at dinner time and all. I saw your truck outside, and I was hoping I might catch you in here."

Sarah was taken aback by the man's formal demeanor. He was typically more gruff and he wasn't known as a man who did a lot of apologizing.

Sarah hadn't seen much of Cinder in the past several months, after buying out all of his raw materials and equipment and hiring most of his employees. He had charged her well below market value for everything and even gave her most of his extra equipment. His only request was for her to owe him a favor, if the time ever came that he needed one.

Favors for men like her father and Cinder were serious business. They meant more than money or possessions and could be called in for just about anything. Now that Cinder was standing in front of her with hat in hand and a serious look on his face, she had a feeling that favor was about to be called in.

Lucas moved over so that the man could sit down next to him facing Sarah. Cinder sat down and placed his hat on the table. He looked over at the tall stranger quizzically then back to Sarah.

"This is my friend Lucas. He came to town visiting for a while, but he's 'good people.'" The term "good people" was a signal to Cinder that he could talk openly about whatever was bothering him without worrying about it being repeated.

"Well, I guess I should just get right to it. I'm afraid I'm going to have to ask you to make good on that marker. I really didn't intend on calling it in so soon, or ever if I could help it."

"That's okay, Mister Cinder. A deal is a deal. What is that you are needing?"

The old man let out a sigh. "I don't know if you heard or not, but my grandson Coal got sent back from the war a few months ago. He got into a firefight with some of them damned old Vietcong, and they blew off two of his fingers. The Army thought he wouldn't be much use without his trigger finger, so they sent him back home. He wasn't happy about me closing down the barrel company, 'cause he didn't have much of a way to make money for his family. You know his girlfriend Violet turned up pregnant just a few weeks after he shipped out, so he now has a new wife and a baby."

He leaned in closer and lowered his voice. "He didn't have a lot of options, so I let him start using my old moonshine still. He started making about thirty jugs of shine every month, which was enough to pay the bills. But he started to get greedy, doubled his batches, and started taking them down to Nashville."

Sarah was starting to get a sick feeling in her stomach. Moonshining was something that was still common in the area, so that wasn't much of a surprise. However, she had kept up with the laws better than most in recent years because of the restrictions that had been put on her company.

The federal government had recently started enforcing new laws that made it a felony to transport illegal liquor across state lines. If Coal was caught selling moonshine in Nashville, that would set him up for at least a few years in the federal pen.

Cinder continued his story, "Well I guess he sold his last batch to some new feller who was in trouble with the feds, and he ratted out Coal. I heard from a deputy friend that they are planning to raid the old shed at the back of my farm in the morning."

Sarah leaned back in her seat. She was starting to get an idea of what he was asking her to do.

"Coal has every penny he has wrapped up in those

bottles of liquor. I don't have any way to transport that big of a load, and I haven't got anywhere safe to store it."

She rubbed the back of her head trying to process everything she had been told. Her gut told her that she should do everything possible to get out of this situation, but she understood that her family's honor was at stake. She had agreed to the favor, so now she was bound to make good on her promise.

She looked at Lucas who was confused by the strange conversation. He probably had some idea that this was an uncomfortable and illegal situation, but he couldn't fully understand the pickle she was in.

"Go get Coal and I'll meet you at the old barn as soon as the sun goes down. I have a place we can store everything until a better option comes up."

The Reluctant Bootleggers

Sarah gripped the steering wheel tight as she maneuvered the large flatbed Ford down an overgrown logging road. The directions to the barn Cinder gave her had led them to the far end of his farm and an area she had never seen. She did not like driving on such a precarious road at night with just the dim headlights to guide her.

She looked over at Lucas, who appeared unfazed by the awkward situation. She had tried to convince him to stay in town and not get mixed up in this mess, but he refused to listen to reason. He seemed almost excited by the idea of helping to move a load of contraband whiskey around the countryside. She made sure to explain the repercussions that they would all face if caught with the illegal booze, but he insisted on helping.

Sarah understood that he was a grown man, making his own decisions, but she would never forgive herself if he were arrested and drummed out of the Marines for helping her out of a jam. This was her favor to repay.

Finally, the road opened into a small clearing and she could see the dilapidated old barn. Cinder's truck was parked out front, and she could see that Cinder and Coal were both wheeling barrels out the front door.

The next part of the task was not going to be easy. Empty oak barrels weighed more than a hundred pounds, but full they were at least five hundred pounds. Cinder had said that Coal still had four barrels capped, and those would be hard to roll up on the truck with only four people. The rest of the booze was bottled in gallon jugs, which would be easier to load.

Sarah backed the truck into position and jumped out. She pulled out the ramp that was designed specifically for loading barrels and locked it into place. The ramp was sturdy, but it had never been tested on full barrels before.

She turned around and waved at Cinder and Coal to get things into motion. "I hope this ramp can support the weight. I guess we'll find out."

Cinder helped his grandson tip one of the barrels onto its side. "Sorry for making you come up the back way. I didn't want anyone seeing you come down the main road in your big truck. I doubt the feds would know about that old logging road."

It took all the strength that both men had, plus Lucas to roll the barrel up the ramp. Sarah stood on the bed of the truck and helped guide the barrel as it reached the top. They positioned it at the front of the bed near the cab and ran back down to start the process again. It took them fifteen minutes to move the four full barrels into place, and they were already exhausted.

Next, they started carrying out boxes of whiskey jugs. In total, they loaded more than forty cases of whiskey. Sarah was starting to understand the magnitude of Coal's investment. He likely had more than three thousand dollars of his money tied up into the massive haul of liquor.

They loaded the last box and started strapping everything down. In the distance, a faint glow from a pair of headlight could be seen on the highway. The vehicle had to be about ten miles out. Everyone stepped up their pace, but there was no need to get too excited about one set of headlights.

Next, they threw a tarp over the load and started weaving ropes through the eyelets. A second and third set of lights popped into view, and panic started to set in. It was rare for one vehicle to come up the road at this time of night. Three vehicles in a line could only mean trouble.

"Forget the tarp for now. Just head down that logging road and keep your lights off. Coal and I will stay back here and create a distraction. We'll meet you over at your farm in a little while."

"Do you remember where the old red barn is at the back of my daddy's farm?"

"Yeah, the one he used to run moonshine out of back in the day?"

"That's the one. Meet us there when you can. We can park the whole truck in the barn for now."

Sarah and Lucas climbed in the truck and headed down the logging road. She tried to go as fast as she could, but the rutted-out road made it difficult to go more than ten miles an hour without bouncing the load around too much.

She finally made it to the smoother gravel road and sped up to forty miles an hour. She could see red and yellow flames glowing in her rear-view mirror and craned her neck back to get a better look. Lucas followed her gaze and turned around in his seat to see the growing flames.

It was clear that Cinder's distraction plan was to set the whole damn barn on fire. That should give the authorities something to concentrate on for a while.

Once they had driven about fifteen miles away, they stopped and finished tying down the tarps. Then they drove the rest of the way to the old red barn at the back of the Blackstone farm.

Sarah asked Lucas to open the large doors, and she drove the truck into the barn. He closed the door behind her, and she shut the truck off and jumped out. Sarah's heart was still racing from her bootleg run, and she was thankful that they hadn't been followed.

She was now standing in near total darkness in the cold, dank building. She walked toward the back of the truck and ran into Lucas. She grabbed him and pulled him in close, wrapping her arms around his mid-section. Then she laid her head against his chest as he rocked her back and forth.

What an odd way to start a relationship she thought to herself. But at least they were already making memories.

A Change of Occupation

It was nearly five in the morning before the sound of a vehicle woke Sarah from her slumber. She was wrapped in Lucas' arms, and they were covered in an old blanket that she had found in the barn. She stood up and peeked out a crack in the door to see Cinder and Coal sitting in the cab of a truck. She opened the door a crack and walked out to meet them.

"I haven't seen this place in at least twenty years. I thought it would be a heap of rotted wood by now."

Sarah smiled at him and slid the large door open. She knew he was really going to be surprised by what he saw next.

Cinder and Coal both stood slack jawed as they saw what was hiding inside the huge barn. There were five large racks filled to the brim with nearly two hundred beautiful new oak barrels.

"Well, I'll be a opossum's uncle. No wonder Elwood was always able to kick my ass on delivery dates. The man must have been sandbagging his whole damn life."

"It was a secret to us a well, until after he died. Apparently, he squirreled away a few barrels every month, and it added up over the years."

Coal walked up and started rubbing on one of the finely crafted barrels. "Damn Sarah, there must be a fortune in here. I can't thank you enough for taking the risk to help me out and showing us this place and all. I know how big of a pickle this puts you in."

"Well, I didn't have much of a choice, Coal. I owed your grandaddy a favor, and I wasn't going to welch on a called marker."

The four of them spent the rest of the morning unloading the boxes of moonshine and stacking them in a corner. They rearranged some of the barrels on the racks so that they could fit the four full barrels in the center of one of the racks where they would be hidden for as long as needed.

They re-loaded the boxes of liquor and tied them down with the tarps. Coal had arranged to sell the whole lot to a buyer in northern Kentucky later that day. He wouldn't get nearly as much as he could have in Tennessee, but it was too risky to try and move the shipment across state lines with the feds still hot on his trail. They would be watching for him to move the liquor out of state to the south, so getting rid of it an hour to the north and still in Kentucky was a much safer option. There was still considerable risk, but at least the punishment would be cut in half if he was caught.

Once the truck was loaded and ready, Coal took off to meet with his buyer leaving Cinder to drive Sarah and Lucas back to the Blackstone workshop. They were all quiet the entire ride, due mostly to sore muscles and lack of sleep.

As they climbed out of the truck, Cinder reached out and touched Sarah's arm. "Sarah, I want you to know your debt to me is paid, and then some. I know I don't have any right to ask this, especially after all you have done, but I was wondering if you might be willing to do another favor for me."

Sarah had a feeling something like this was coming. She climbed out of the truck and leaned in the passenger side window. "I will figure something out. Victor and Bill won't like it, but I will bring them around. Just tell Coal to show up on Monday morning. We can use all the good barrel makers we can get."

Angry Brother

It had been nearly two weeks since the bootleg run, and things were starting to normalize at the Blackstone Oak Barrel Company. Bill had not been very happy about having to find a job for Coal, who had been his biggest rival for so many years. He was even less happy to find out that both Cinder and Coal knew about the company's reserve stash of barrels.

However, Bill came around quickly once he saw how hard Coal worked, and even took some of his advice on how to change a few of their equipment settings. The two men were working together on completing maintenance on one of the steel cutters when Victor came marching into the workshop.

Victor glared over at Bill, who just shrugged his shoulders. Then he looked over at Coal before crinkling up his nose and marching into the office. Sarah was sitting behind the desk looking over the books, while Lucas sat in the corner carving out flowers on a wooden box he had recently made in the workshop.

Victor stomped up to the desk in a huff. "What the hell is Coal doing out in the workshop?"

"Well hello brother, how was your trip to Florida? I can see that it must have been very relaxing."

"Don't you play me like that. What the hell is going on? And who the hell is that?" He said pointing over at Lucas, who was now looking up with a chisel in his hand.

"Well, dear brother, if you must know, that is my boyfriend, Lucas. And as for Coal, Old Man Cinder asked me to hire him as a favor. The man has a new wife and a baby to care for, and I felt like it was the right thing to do since we did run him out of job and all."

Victor was still steaming, but he wasn't quite sure how to take the brutal honesty coming at him.

Sarah stood up and closed the books. "All the

vendors are paid up to date. Bill has the order list for the rest of the month, and I will be making a deposit at the bank this afternoon. Make sure to pick up the payroll checks on Friday, and order another shipment of wood on Monday."

"What are you talking about? Where are you going?"

"Lucas has to be in California in a couple weeks, and we are going to take a road trip together. I will fly back to Nashville after the trip, and it would be kind of you to pick me up at the airport. I'll call to check in on you in a couple days."

Sarah handed him the ledger and the keys before signaling to Lucas that it was time to go. Lucas walked over and shook Victor's hand. "It was very nice meeting you."

Lucas had to move quick to catch up to Sarah, who was already outside the workshop and heading to the pickup.

As Sarah and Lucas headed back into town, Sarah could see a broad smile on Lucas' face. "What are you grinning about over there?"

"Boyfriend, huh?"

Sarah blushed and turned her head away. "I figured, any man willing to commit a felony for me, is probably worth keeping around for a while."

Train Ride to Missouri

Sarah and Lucas were sitting together on a train

bench. The whistle blew as the engine roared into motion.

"So where are we going to visit first?" Sarah asked as she leaned her head on his shoulder.

"Well, I guess I should probably go home to Missouri for a few days. My mother is really going to get a kick out of you."

Sarah smiled and nodded her head. She had never been to Missouri, but how different could it be from Kentucky. Both states were known for producing hillbillies and moonshine. She figured she would fit in just fine.

CANCER – PART 4

"No one loves the messenger who brings bad news."

– Sophocles

The Final Verdict

Sarah could tell that Lucas was angry. This time it wasn't part of the grieving process; he was genuinely angry. Angry at the surgeons and doctors. Angry at the test results. Angry at her for not finding a way to get better. He was even angry at God for putting them in this situation.

She wanted to comfort him, but she didn't know how. Besides, she was more than a little angry herself. She had done everything possible to beat her illness.

She had gone through a double mastectomy and had two additional surgeries to remove more tumors in her lymph nodes. She had suffered through a rough cycle of radiation and three cycles of chemotherapy. She had changed her diet, changed her exercise routine, and even changed her sleeping habits.

There was no way to tell how much all these efforts had impacted the cancer cells raging inside her body. They had likely slowed the progression and gave her more time, but they had not come close to curing or even stopping the disease.

Lucas gripped the steering wheel as tightly as he could and closed his eyes. He kept repeating the words, "Why? Why? Why?"

Sarah placed her hand on his thigh and squeezed it to let him know she was with him. Her touch brought him out of his trance, and he looked at her with a flash of anger still showing in his eyes. Her reaction must have alerted him to his selfish behavior.

"I'm sorry, honey. I just wasn't ready to hear all of that. The doctor just kept talking and everything he said was just… Well, it was just damn horrible."

Sarah smiled at him. "I know, but we can't focus on that now. We have to be strong for the boys and we have to cherish the time we have left together."

Lucas leaned over and hugged his wife, and they both cried together for a few minutes.

This visit had been the worst for Sarah since her initial diagnosis. She had stopped all her treatments just over a month ago in order for the radiation and chemo drugs to leave her body. Once those were out of her system, she was scheduled for an MRI to determine whether or not the cancer had stopped or continued to grow.

There had even been hope that the cancer might have gone into partial or complete remission. All the tumors had been removed, and the oncologist had enrolled her in the latest experimental treatments. Lucas had especially convinced himself that they were going to receive good news that morning.

From the moment the doctor walked into the room, Sarah understood that the news was going to be bad. She grabbed Lucas' arm so that they could support each other as they sat quietly and listened to the prognosis.

The doctor explained that the cancer in her chest and lymph nodes had slowed a bit, but it was clear that it was not going to stop. To make matters worse, the cancerous cells in her lungs were now growing at an alarming rate.

The conversation was slow and contained lots of detail.

The doctor told them he wanted Sarah to have one last tumor removed that had appeared on the side of her chest, followed by a moderate dose of chemotherapy. He made it clear that the measures were no longer meant as a cure, but simply as a way to buy time and to make her more comfortable.

It was obvious that the doctor was leading up to a climax, and Sarah finally pushed him for a timeline. In the past, the doctor would not give an estimate of how much time she had left to live. He would simply say that it was too soon for such thoughts because there were so many options left to explore.

This time was different. He leaned in and said that if they moved forward with the surgery and one more round of chemo that she would probably live another three to five months.

The news was devastating. Neither her nor Lucas reacted right away. Instead, they just excused themselves from the office and headed to the truck. They wanted to be as far away from the awful news as possible.

They continued sitting in the truck, not sure of what to do. The boys would be waiting for them at the house, and they were not ready to face them yet. Plus, they still needed time to process everything.

Sarah turned to her husband and smiled. "Now that the trees have started to turn, we should take a drive down a country road and look at all the pretty fall foliage."

Lucas nodded his head and headed out to the edge of town. They drove around the scenic roads staring quietly out the window. After a while Lucas decided it was time to start talking about the elephant in the room. "What do we tell the boys?"

"We tell them the truth. We tell them the cancer is still there, and we are continuing to fight. They don't need to know about the timeline or any of that. Knowing that it will happen soon would just make it harder on them. It's better for them to hold onto hope until the end."

Lucas nodded. She could tell that he wasn't looking forward to telling the boys. But not having to tell them she had less than five months to live would make the conversation a little easier.

"Do you think that is selfish of me?"

"No. I think it makes you a good mother. It is better that they spend their time with you concentrating on happy thoughts. We will tell them only what we need to. They will understand when the time comes."

Sarah scooted over in the bench seat and leaned her head against his shoulder.

"Now let's stop talking about cancer. Why don't you go buy me a strawberry shake while my taste buds still work?"

"Yes, dear. Right away."

KILLING MONSTERS

"We don't tell our children stories so they know monsters are real. We tell them stories so they know monsters can be slain."

– Author Unknown

Winter 2005

Starting the Journey

Sarah Blackstone-Fosterman sat in her Jeep Wrangler outside the gates of the prison as the rain fell hard. She gripped the steering wheel tightly staring blankly at the water beading on the windshield.

After Katie's death she had occasionally thought that there might have been other victims. Other innocent little girls. Those thoughts were pushed aside in order to allow her to tend to her own family's pain and loss. Besides, that was a matter for the authorities.

The district attorney had turned Jim Powers' life upside down looking for evidence to tie him to Katie's murder. If there was evidence of other girls they would have surely found it. But she knew this was a lie. They had barely found enough proof to tie him to Katie's death.

The only evidence they had found was on her body, which was uncovered in that old barn. Even finding her body had been a stroke of luck. She had been buried in the dirt in the barn, and a hound dog had signaled on it. Only a few of the search parties even had dogs, and it was by God's hand that one of those parties was searching that particular farm that afternoon.

Jim Powers' DNA was found under two of Katie's fingernails. She had fought hard until the end. But until now Sarah thought she had only fought one man.

Jim had asked her to visit him at the prison, and she had come because she needed to see his face for some reason. He did not talk to her at first. Instead, he just cried. Then he picked up the phone and said two crushing sentences. "I was not alone. I just delivered the packages."

Then he passed the piece of paper under the glass tray and left the room. Sarah waited until she was in the Jeep before looking at the note. The small piece of paper showed three names. She knew exactly what the names meant, but she did not know what to do about them.

She had never even considered that there were other men involved. The police never brought forth any suspects. The FBI had even been involved during the search, but they had never talked about anyone other than Jim after the arrest had been made.

Looking at the names again, she could understand why. She did not recognize two of the names, Jack Picker and Tom Paulson. The third name she did recognize, and it made her skin crawl, Payton Becvar. He was one of lead investigators on Katie's case.

It was clear to her now that Payton had been responsible for mishandling the evidence and had intentionally botched the interrogation process in order to get Jim set free.

She began to tear up as she thought of the

implication this news would have on her family. She knew immediately that she could never tell them. Lucas would be devastated, and her sons would become instant vigilantes. They would throw away their lives to make the three men on the piece of paper pay for their evils.

This was now her secret. Her burden to bear. And she had no intention of letting these men continue hurting little girls.

Private Investigation

Sarah was surprised at how much information could be found on the internet when searching people's records. A quick search on Payton Becvar gave his complete bio. He was born in Fort Smith, Arkansas in 1972, where he grew up until going to Arkansas State University in Jonesboro. He then moved to Missouri and joined the police force as an officer for five years before passing his detective's exam. He had now been a detective for nearly ten years.

She continued digging into his records trying to find a connection with the other two names. She started in his hometown of Fort Smith, but there was little information about Payton's early years. She saw one photo of him as a young man in an article about his father, who was also an officer. The photo showed Payton standing by his father as he received a commendation for saving a young girl's life.

Not finding anything related to the other names in Fort Smith, she moved on to searching the university records. She spent hours sifting through records from 1991-1996, not knowing exactly what years he attended the school. She found nothing on the University website or any searches about the University of Arkansas.

She tried the names of all the other men, including Jim Powers. Nothing came up at the university. Then she moved on to the Jonesboro newspaper. She knew it was a longshot, but she was running out of options.

The paper had a remarkably useful search feature, and she got a hit when typing in Payton Becvar. The search popped up a picture and cutline that showed Payton and Jim Powers standing with a group of other men in fishing gear. The photo was taken at Greers Ferry Lake and showed five smiling men holding up stringers full of largemouth bass. The cutline stated that the team of men had won a tournament. She saw the names reading left to right: Jim Powers, Tom Paulson, Payton Becvar, Jackson Picker, and Nolan Foxman.

The sight of the names on the cutline made the hair on her neck raise. She had found them. In the matter of only a few hours she had located pictures of the men.

She spent the entire night searching through every record she could find on the three men. She discovered that Tom Paulson lived in Little Rock. He was a real estate agent and had his picture plastered all over his website. Like all the other men, he was in his late forties. He had a full head of brown hair that was slicked back. He wore a blue suit in all his photos. She cringed as she looked at one photo of the man standing with his family, including his wife and a little girl who looked to be about fourteen. Sarah looked closely at the little girl who seemed to be forcing a smile. She had to wonder what life had been like for that child.

Jackson Picker was just as easy to find. He was now living in Branson as a chef at one of the restaurants in the downtown area. His picture was also shown on the website. He was a balding black man who smiled broadly in all his pictures. Even though he was wearing a thick black chef coat in all the images, she could tell he had a round belly.

She found out more information about Jackson when reading a review of the restaurant. It turns out he had gotten a divorce a few years ago. The reviewer also mentioned that he had lost a daughter not too long ago. She searched more and found out that his eleven year old daughter had drowned in Greers Ferry Lake after swimming at a cabin owned by Payton Becvar.

Wanting to be thorough, she also spent time searching for Nolan Foxman. It didn't take long for her to find an obituary for the man. Nolan had died five years ago in a boating accident, again on Greers Ferry Lake. He was survived by his wife Tammy and two daughters who would have been nine and twelve at the time of his death.

Sarah realized that a pattern was quickly

developing. She did not need any more convincing that these men were monsters, but she wanted to make certain before deciding on her next steps. She did one last search and printed out a name and address for Tammy Foxman in Little Rock, Arkansas.

Weekend Trip

It took little convincing to get Lucas on board with taking a weekend trip to Little Rock. Sarah had a friend named Veronica who worked at the Rock Town Distillery, and she had been trying to get Sarah to visit the small liquor operation for several years.

Veronica was the purchasing agent at the distillery, and she had purchased several small batch barrels from Sarah over the years. They had struck up a friendship years ago while attending a trade show.

Lucas and Sarah drove the five hours to Little Rock on Friday and met Veronica and her husband for dinner that evening. The next morning, Lucas and Sarah took a tour of the distillery before Lucas left with Veronica's husband for a round of golf at a course located a few miles out of town. Sarah had arranged for the golf outing so that it would give her enough time to find and visit with Tammy Foxman.

Sarah entered the address into her phone and followed the winding roads to a suburb on the edge of town. She pulled up in front of the brick house and waited a second to collect her thoughts before getting out. She had been trying to determine what to say to the lady; what questions to ask.

She thought about posing as a reporter or maybe an investigator. But that seemed risky and felt wrong. She decided she would stay with the truth but divulge as little information as possible.

Walking up to the door, she decided to knock instead of ringing the doorbell. A few seconds later a middle-aged woman appeared holding a large glass of wine. It was only noon on a Saturday, but Sarah had a suspicion that this wasn't the woman's first full glass of the day.

"Missus Foxman?"

"Yes, I'm Tammy Foxman. What can I do for you?"

"My name is Sarah Blackstone-Fosterman."

"I saw you on TV. You're that little girl's grandma. The one who was killed in Missouri."

The lady opened the door and led Sarah over to the couch. She put her wine glass on the counter and used a tissue to wipe the red stain off her lips.

"I'm sorry to bother you. I was just hoping to ask you a couple questions about Jim Powers."

The lady stopped moving and didn't turn around for a few seconds. She turned and sat down in a chair not making immediate eye contact. "I'm afraid I don't know much about Jim Powers. He was an acquaintance of my late husband, but I only saw him a couple of times."

Sarah knew she had to choose her words carefully. "I understand. I'm just grasping at straws. I found a picture in the Jonesboro newspaper of Jim Powers with your husband and a few other men. I was just hoping maybe you might have known them better."

"You saw them in a picture?"

Sarah looked in her purse and pulled out a printout of the picture from the newspaper showing the five men at the fishing tournament. Tammy looked at the photo and started shaking. Tears filled her eyes, and she sat silently looking at the image. Sarah waited patiently.

"I should have never let Nolan take the girls to that lake. They had no business being at that cabin with those horrible men."

The words came as a shock to Sarah. "Your daughters were at the cabin when your husband drowned?"

Tammy looked up. It seemed like she just realized that Sarah was still in the room with her. She grabbed a tissue and wiped her eyes. She handed the picture back to Sarah. "I'm sorry, but I can't be of any help to you. It was such a long time ago."

"But Missus Foxman, Tammy, I am just trying to figure out what is going on here. What might have really happened to my granddaughter."

"I'm really sorry about all that, but I must ask you to leave. I have to an engagement I can't be late for this afternoon." She stood up and started walking toward the door.

Sarah felt her blood pressure rising. She needed more answers. "Is there really nothing you can tell me? I don't understand why you can't just talk to me."

"I must insist that you leave. I really can't be late."

Sarah stared at the woman. Realizing that she had gotten all that she could, she grabbed her purse and walked past her. As she reached the door, the woman put her hand on her shoulder.

"I really am sorry, but you must understand. Those men in that picture, they are not the kind of men that you talk about. I have two daughters. Please don't ever come back to this house. Erase our names from your phone, your computer, your life."

The woman's voice was not angry. Instead, she was pleading. Her hand trembled as she spoke. "Jim Powers is a bad man, but he is nothing compared to the evil that will fall on your family if those other three men find out you have been asking questions about them."

Sarah nodded and walked out the door. She climbed in her Jeep and looked back at the house. She could see Tammy looking out the window. She wasn't looking at the Jeep but instead scanning the other houses in the area looking for witnesses.

On the ride back to the hotel, Sarah found herself breathing hard and sweating. Her worst fears had been confirmed. The men in the photo had now been confirmed to be monsters.

She was certain that at least one of them had been involved in Katie's abduction and murder. It did not matter if it was only one or all three. It was clear that they were all monsters.

She could not rid the world of all its evil. She knew she did not have long left in this life. But even in her weakened state she might have the ability to rid the world of three monsters. At least she was going to try like hell.

Locked and Loaded

It had only been a week since Sarah and Lucas returned from their trip to Little Rock. Lucas had gone back to work at his shop helping his sons fill a large order of wooden pews for the Catholic church.

Sarah was in the shed behind the house where her small woodworking shop and forge was located. She finished bending a few metal bands to fit around a small oak barrel before shutting off the propane tank and removing her heavy leather gloves. In her weakened state, she could only work on one or two small barrel a day.

She looked out the window to make sure she was alone, then locked the door to the shed and went to her gun safe on the back wall. It was a midsize safe that only held a few of her personal weapons. She entered the combination and opened the door to reveal a small assortment of rifles, shotguns, and pistols.

She took out the largest rifle in the safe and sat it on the nearby table and looked it over. It had been several months since she had shot the weapon. Ever since her breast cancer diagnosis, other priorities had taken over, but she did miss shooting the precision firearm.

For several decades, Sarah had been a member of a

long-range rifle team. She had won several local and even a few national shooting matches. She had retired from competitive shooting about eight years ago, but she still loved going to the range as often as possible.

She grabbed a rag and a bottle of gun oil and started to clean and inspect the weapon. The rifle was a gift from Lucas and her sons nearly fifteen years ago. It had long been a dream of hers to own a purpose-built precision rifle from Accurate Ordinance. It was chambered in 6.5mm Creedmoor, which was her favorite caliber.

The rifle was custom in every way including a Manners T4-A stock, Stiller TAC 30 action, and picatinny rails embedded in optimal locations. It was topped by a U.S. Optics SN-3 3.2-17x44mm scope with T-Pal Mil Scale GAP.

Lucas always made fun of her when she rattled off the specs on the rifle and scope to their friends. She knew that most people would have no idea what she was talking about, but it was her prized possession, and she had no qualms about showing it off.

She finished cleaning the rifle and placed it in the hard case she used to transport the weapon. She stored the case and rifle in the safe.

She opened her ammo can and looked through the plastic boxes of custom ammunition. Her youngest son was skilled at hand loading ammunition, which was an important part of being a successful competitive shooter. Factory ammo was fine for plinking, but to shoot quarters at over 500 yards took the perfect recipe of gun powder and lead.

Sarah looked through the boxes of ammo that her son had made for her and found the three that she wanted. The tops were marked with five hundred yards, seven hundred fifty yards, and one thousand yards. These were the most common distances that Sarah had shot in competitions.

She pulled out a small shooting bag and placed the three boxes containing twenty rounds each into the center compartment. She checked the side pockets to make sure her range finder, ear protection, and shooting glasses were in place. She also threw in an extra bottle of gun oil and a couple of cleaning towels before zipping up the bag. The bag was placed in the safe by the rifle case, and she closed and locked the door. She was confident everything was ready.

After her preparations in the shed, Sarah took a shower and prepared herself for her afternoon visit to the hospital. She was at the end of a four-week run of chemo and radiation therapy, and only had one more day of treatments.

The treatments had gone as well as they could. She had become weaker and weaker with each passing day, but that was to be expected.

She also knew that the weakness would likely get much worse over the next few days, but the doctors expected her to feel much better about a week after her final session. But the real question was how long her strength would hold out.

She understood that the treatments were not meant to be a cure. They were just a way to slow down the stage four metastatic breast cancer that was rotting out her chest cavity and seeping deeper into her lungs.

Alone Time

The first two days after her final chemo and radiation treatment were the hardest. Sarah endured more pain than she had ever experienced. Even the natural births of her two sons couldn't compare to the sustained agony she felt. By the third day, the pain had dulled but the nausea persisted. She hadn't eaten anything for days, and Lucas threatened to take her back to the hospital.

On day four, her appetite returned a little. Lucas tried feeding her all her favorite foods, but everything tasted like cardboard. She settled by eating blueberries, which at least had a pleasant texture. She also drank a couple protein shakes throughout the day, which helped to cool her raw throat.

By day five, she felt well enough to take a walk around the neighborhood. Then on day six, she even worked in the forge for an hour with Lucas standing six feet away at all times. He looked ready to pounce at even the slightest stumble.

That evening the whole family came over, and they all ate dinner together. Sarah stayed up until nine, then Lucas started ushering everyone out of the house. That night Lucas helped her change the bandages around her chest. Her wounds from a recent surgery to remove a small tumor under her armpit were healing nicely. She now only needed four wraps of gauze and there was no blood spotting on the cloth.

The next several days continued to go well, as Sarah grew stronger. She worked in the forge for a couple hours each day, careful not to overdo it. After two weeks, she decided to test herself and worked six hours at the forge. She was able to get through the test but had to take a three-hour nap that afternoon. She wished she could have gone longer. Her limitations would add at least a day to her itinerary and make it harder to convince Lucas to let her go.

She made sure to keep Lucas updated on her health every day. She needed him to feel comfortable with her traveling on her own for a while. She waited until dinner that night to start the conversation.

She told him she needed to get away for a few days. Between the doctor visits, family visits, and visits from friends, she was feeling suffocated. She hadn't had more than a day to herself since her diagnosis, and her health was finally to the point where she felt well enough to travel on her own. She had been inspired by their trip to Arkansas and had always wanted to visit the state's famous hot springs. She had found a relaxing destination called the Arlington Resort Hotel and Spa.

Lucas was resistant at first, but it was clear that his wife was set on making the trip. At first, he insisted on driving her to the hotel and picking her up when she was done. She convinced him that the drive was just as important as the resort to her. He knew how much she liked taking road trips in her Jeep, and she promised to make frequent stops during the five-hour drive.

The next day, she pulled her Wrangler into the shed and started packing. She made sure no one was around when she removed the rifle case and shooting bag from the safe and stored it in the locker Lucas had built for her under the back bench seat. She tossed a small suitcase in the back, along with a case of water, some protein bars, and a large bag of gummy bears. She also threw in a blanket and pillow.

That afternoon she went to the library and used a computer for an hour to send out a few emails and print out some addresses and directions. She met Lucas for an early dinner, and they both were back and ready for bed before nine.

The next morning, she slept in until eight. After a nice breakfast with Lucas, her sons Mark and Paul came over to try and talk her out of making the trip. She hugged them both and told them not to worry. She would only be gone five days, and she would call them all at least once every day to check in.

She was on the road by eleven, heading south toward Arkansas. She was running on nervous energy, so she was able to make the first three hours of the trip without stopping. She fueled up at a truck stop, then took a short nap before continuing on with her drive. She arrived at the resort outside Little Rock at a little after six.

She was exhausted from the drive, too exhausted. She knew she was going to need to be stronger over the next few days if she was ever going to pull off her plan. After checking in, she ordered room service and called Lucas and her sons to let them know she had made it to the hotel.

She only ate half her dinner before crawling into bed.

Friday – Tom Paulson

The decorative granite tile on the bathroom floor felt cool under Sarah's legs. She had been kneeling there for nearly twenty minutes. Her stomach was empty now, and she had finally stopped dry heaving. The nausea was mostly gone now.

She had gone through enough cancer treatment to know that the knots in her stomach were not from her illness. She had spent weeks researching and planning out what she needed to accomplish over the next four days. Logistically and physically, she felt prepared. It was the mental part she was having a problem with now.

She had never taken a life before, and she wasn't sure she would be able to do it. Throughout her life, she had considered herself to be a good person, and hurting people certainly wasn't something that good people did. But this was different. This was a matter of survival. She wasn't in this for vengeance. This was a matter of stopping an atrocity. She wasn't going to be killing men. She was going to be exterminating monsters.

A hot shower helped to sooth her frazzled nerves. She pulled her hair up into a ponytail and dressed in loose fitting jeans and a sweatshirt. She felt much better now that she was up and running. She thought about eating a protein bar but decided to wait a bit in case her stomach started churning again.

She left the hotel at just after one o'clock and jumped in her Jeep. She took the small notepad out of her bag and looked at the address and directions she had printed out. Even after hitting a little traffic, the drive took less than an hour.

She arrived at her destination at a little before two, and she had two hours to scope out the area. She drove down the two lane blacktop road until she saw a twenty acre plot of land on the right side of the road. There was a nice ranch style house in the center. The "For Sale" sign in the yard confirmed that she was in the correct location. A headshot of Tom Paulson's smiling mug could be seen from road.

She drove past the house and took the first left onto a gravel road. There was a powerline access road less than two blocks in that turned back to the left. The satellite map of the area had shown this access road, and she was glad to find that it was more hidden and wooded that it looked on the computer screen. She travelled along the dirt road a few hundred yards until she could see the house across the way.

She drove further down the dirt road until she got to the top of the hill. Other than the house, there was nothing but farmland and forest in all directions. She turned the vehicle around and drove slowly down the hill, stopping at several locations to determine the best vantage point to the house. She found a small clearing between two cedar trees and pulled the Jeep off the road and into the clearing. She was pressed against the branches of the tree, which helped to hide her white Wrangler from view.

She couldn't see the blacktop road below her, which was good. It meant that people on the road also couldn't see her. She also couldn't see the gravel road below from her position. It was unnerving to be sitting out in the open during broad daylight, but this was better concealment than she had expected.

Sarah rolled down the right side back window and climbed into the back seat of the Jeep. She removed her rifle from the case and the grabbed the box of ammo marked 750 yards then pulled the range finder out of the bag and pointed it at the house. She decided against wearing the hearing protection because she wanted to be able to hear any approaching vehicles.

She measured the distance to the front door which was just under 780 yards. She measured out several other points around the house. The garage door was 730 yards. The circle driveway in front of the house was 715 yards. The mailbox by the road was 614 yards.

The sky was filled with white puffy clouds that helped hide the sun. The wind was blowing east to west at less than five miles per hour. It was a perfect day for shooting.

She filled a magazine with five rounds and slipped it into the rifle. She then chambered a round and engaged the safety. The pillow and blanket were still sitting in the back, and she pulled them out and tucked them under the rifle for support. She popped the flip caps on the scope and positioned herself behind the rifle lying across the back seat in the prone position. She had a perfect view of the house. She could easily swing the barrel enough to reach every corner of the property, and at a magnification of seventeen she could clearly see the doorknob which she had calculated at 760 yards.

Once satisfied that things were in order, she set her watch for 3:45. Sarah had set the meeting with Tom Paulson for four in the afternoon using a fake email address she created. She used the assumed name of Mack Gunderman to pretend to be a prospective buyer who was considering making a cash offer on some property in the area. She had searched through the two dozen properties that Tom had listed on his website and found the most remote listing he had available. Even more convenient was the fact that the property owners had recently moved to Florida, so the house was vacant.

She was surprised to be awoken by the sound of her watch beeping at her. She cleaned the sleep from her eyes and looked through the scope at the house. There were still no vehicles in sight.

She could see her hand shake slightly so she ate a protein bar and drank some water. She got back into position behind the scope and tried her best to steady her nerves. The shaking had stopped, but now she could hear her heart beating in her ears. She had to calm down.

A few minutes later a gray sedan turned into the driveway and made its way up to the house. Tom was right on time. She waited until he parked the car and got out of the vehicle. She verified that he was alone, as he walked up to the door and rang the doorbell. Thankfully, no one answered, and he used the code to unlock the door and walked in.

Sarah let her long-range shooting instincts take over. She started her shallow breathing exercises. She let her hands and arms go limp and relaxed her neck and shoulder muscles. This helped to slow down her heart rate. Her vision narrowed as she focused in on the doorknob through the scope.

She checked the wind again, which was still blowing at a soft five miles an hour. She checked her elevation, which should be perfect for these conditions. During a competition she would have no problem putting five rounds into a three-inch group under these conditions. Today she did not need a tight group. She just needed one very accurate shot.

Ten minutes later Tom reappeared in the doorway. He closed the door and sat down on the porch facing her direction. She knew this was going to be her best opportunity. Looking through the scope, she could see the fat double Windsor knot on his bright red tie.

She started the routine again from the top. Check the sun. Check the windage. Check the elevation. Check the distance. Slow the breathing. Slow the heart rate. Relax the arms. Relax the hands. Relax the neck. Relax the shoulders. Find the mark. Focus on the Windsor Knot. Breath in. Breath out. Squeeze the trigger... Direct hit.

The sound of the loud rifle reverberated throughout the vehicle causing her ears to ring. She looked through the scope again and could see that the man was slumped over on the porch with a pool of blood forming. Convinced he was dead, she laid the rifle in the seat and covered it with the blanket.

She jumped into the front seat, fired up the engine, and pulled up the dirt road. She turned onto the gravel road looking everywhere for cars. She continued on to the blacktop road and turned right, still not seeing any cars. She slowed down as she passed in front of the house. She could see Tom's car from the road but could not see him lying on the porch.

The sound of a rifle being fired in this part of the country probably wouldn't draw much attention, so it was hard to say how long it would take for someone to discover him on that porch.

She sped up after passing the house and drove nearly thirty minutes before finding a secluded area to stop. She quickly packed up the rifle and shooting bag before continuing her drive back to the resort.

As soon as she made it to her room, she kicked off her shoes and laid down in the bed. Her entire body was numb and she could hear a slight ringing in her ears. She had still not processed what had happened. What she had done. She thought she would feel more fear, more guilt, more sadness, but right now all she felt was numbness.

She laid in the bed staring at the ceiling. Then she started to cry. She wasn't sure why, but she knew it wasn't going to stop any time soon.

Saturday – Jackson Picker

Sarah stayed in bed until after noon the next day. She still felt numb, but the ramifications of her actions had started to reverberate in her mind. When she closed her eyes, she could see a looping replay of the shot slamming into the base of Tom's neck.

The scene wasn't accurate, and she knew it. The memory was screwed and enhanced. She could see a large puff of blood around him. His eyes would go wide with surprise. She knew that had never happened. Her mind was creating details, horrible details.

The only benefit was that the nausea was gone. She still felt anxious, but she was surprisingly hungry. She hadn't eaten much more than a protein bar in the last thirty-six hours. Room service brought up a tray of food. Her taste and sense of smell were starting to return, which made the prospect of eating even more appealing. She finished off a whole piece of chicken breast, some vegetables, and a chunk of bread.

Having a full belly also made it easier for her to rest, and she took another nap. She awoke at five in the afternoon, feeling refreshed. She was thankful that her health was holding up better today. She was going to need even more energy for the next stage in her plan. She had a six-hour round trip in her future, along with a long break in between.

She called Lucas and her sons to check in. She could tell that they were still worried about her, but she assured them that she was doing fine. She made sure to tell them about the wonderful resort, tasty food, and beautiful scenery. These things were all true, even though she hadn't really taken much time to enjoy them.

She stopped by the counter on the way out of the hotel to purchase a couple diet Cokes. She also asked for suggestions for local restaurants. She knew it was silly to even try to setup an alibi, but it was worth the small effort.

She jumped in the Jeep and headed north toward Branson. The drive was peaceful, but a little taxing. By the time she pulled into downtown Branson she had a slight headache. She pulled out the bag of gummy bears hoping that a little sugar would help.

The restaurant she was looking for was just ahead, and she pulled into the parking lot and circled behind the building. A group of eight cars lined the back of the lot, and she could see a chef in uniform heading toward a door at the back.

She circled back around the building and stopped at the far end of the lot looking for vantage points. There were not a lot of good options. A high retaining wall at the back of the building blocked off the area, which meant she would need to find a position on the sides. But those options were narrow.

To make matters worse, the door leading into the restaurant was inset and shielded by an awning. She had hoped to have a shot from that angle, but it was clear that the door was not going to be an option. She looked down the line of cars and decided that was her only choice. To the right of the restaurant was a hillside that led up to a second restaurant followed by the back of a hotel parking lot.

She exited the restaurant area and headed up the hill to the hotel parking lot. She drove around to the back and found a spot at the far end of the lot. From this position she could see all eight cars below her. It was a steep angle, but it would provide a clear line of sight to anyone clearing the canopy from the back of the restaurant and walking to their car.

She looked around the parking lot, which was only a quarter full of cars. It was the slow season in Branson, so it was doubtful that many more guests would arrive. Still, she felt very exposed in the lot. This was going to be the trickiest shot to pull off, and she wasn't certain she was even going to be able to go through with it at this location.

Sitting in a more vulnerable spot, she decided to wait to take out the rifle but grabbed the shooting bag and removed the range finder. She pointed it at the first car in the parking lot and saw that it was 483 yards. She then pointed it at the car furthest from her position which was 515 yards. She put the range finder away and took out the box of shells marked 500 yards.

She sat anxiously in the back seat for over an hour waiting for the restaurant to close. Every sound in the parking lot made her jump. She was thankful that no new cars had pulled into the lot; however, one man did come out to get something from his truck at one point.

Even in the somewhat secluded spot, she was still in the center of town. She was taking a huge risk. If there was more time, she would follow her target home instead. Maybe even come back tomorrow and look over the area during the light of day. But those were not options. She had put things into motion when she killed Tom Paulson, and news of his death would soon reach the other two men.

At a little after ten, she pulled the rifle out of the case and set it up the same as before. She waited a while before rolling down the back window using the manual crank. Her dark tinted windows had hidden her from view of anyone walking by, but now she was exposed.

She looked through the scope at the line of cars and was discouraged by the lack of light. She could see about half the cars clearly, but a few were in shadows. At around ten thirty, the first couple of workers came out of the back entrance and headed for their vehicles. She swayed the rifle back and forth looking at their faces. They were both men, but clearly not Jackson.

Her heart was racing, and she realized that she needed to go over her checklist again because she was not going to have much time when Jackson did appear. There was no wind, so windage was at zero.

The elevation was set for 500 yards, but she dialed it down a bit because of the steep grade.

Her headache had worsened, mainly because of her elevated heart rate. She felt a throbbing pain at the base of her neck, which she knew was because of her tight muscles and nerves.

The two men drove out of the parking lot. One of the cars was in the darkest spot, which gave her some hope. She swayed the scope back to the awning and waited. Three women appeared next. They were talking and laughing as two of the women got into one car and the other climbed into an old pickup truck. Just as she was getting ready to move the scope back toward the building a blinding light shone through the window behind her.

Sarah rolled off the rifle and onto the floorboard. She quickly laid the blanket over the rifle and peeked out the window. An old man and woman got out of a sedan and slowly unloaded their luggage. She watched as they entered the hotel room. The whole event took less than ten minutes, but it felt like an eternity to Sarah.

Her heart was racing again. She could only hope that the couple would not need to return to the car again to get more items. She waited a couple more minutes before removing the blanket and climbing back into the prone position. Her heart sank as she looked through the scope. There were now only two cars left in the lot.

Had she missed him? She had to hope that, as the head chef, he would be the last to leave. Doubt started to set in again. It was not a guarantee that he was even there today. He was the chef and owner, but that didn't mean he worked that day. What if he had received news about Tom Paulson? What if he had taken a sick day? What if he had gone home early?

She closed her eyes and shook her head. None of that mattered right now. There were still two cars left. If one of them was his she needed to be ready. The sight of another person walking out the door brought her back to attention. She pulled in tighter on the rifle. It was a man wearing a white coat. He was black but looked too thin to be Jackson. She concentrated on the back of his head. She could see thick black hair, definitely not Jackson. She watched as he got into his car and drove away.

Now that there was only one car in the parking lot, she was more confident that she could take the shot if the opportunity presented itself. She focused in on the driver's side mirror using it at her target mark. She adjusted the elevation by raising it one click. The lighting was not as bright as she hoped it would be.

She swung the rifle back to the awning and saw the flash of a black coat appear. She held her breath and pushed her eye in closer to the scope. Then she saw it again. There was definitely someone at the door, likely locking it up for the night. A second later, a black man appeared wearing a black chef's coat and white hat. As he walked toward the car, he removed his hat revealing a bald head. She was ninety percent sure it was Jackson, but she needed to see his face.

She kept the crosshairs centered on his head as he

walked across the parking lot. At one point he stopped and looked back at the restaurant before continuing on. She had a perfect shot from this angle, but she still needed to see his face.

He got to the car and removed his keys. He worked the key fob to unlock the doors, still not looking up. He grabbed the handle, and she held her breath again. She was going to miss her chance, but she just couldn't pull the trigger until she saw his face.

The man suddenly let go of the door handle and started feeling around on his coat pockets. He found what he was looking for and held his cell phone up to his ear. She watched as he talked to someone on the phone. It was obviously an intense conversation. She could tell by the way he started swinging his arms and grabbing at his bald head.

At one point he looked up, right at in her direction. She had her confirmation. It was Jackson, there was no doubt about it. She focused in on his chest. If it weren't for the angle she would go for a head shot at this distance. But a chest shot gave less room for error.

She hesitated a bit longer. She wanted him to finish the call first. But she was afraid he was going to get in the car. She saw him grab the door handle and panicked. She focused in quickly and fired off a hasty shot. It hit him in the chest, but he had turned before she shot, and she wasn't sure if it had hit him in the heart.

She let the scope rock back into position, then circled the rifle barrel around until she could see him lying on the ground. He wasn't dead. He was grabbing onto his left shoulder writhing in pain. She quickly ejected the empty shell and chambered a fresh round. She aimed the rifle again, this time putting the crosshairs on the man's chin. She took a quick breath in and out, firing at the end of the exhale.

This time, there was no doubt that she hit her mark. She quickly rolled out of the back and jumped into the driver's seat. She started the vehicle and slammed the selector into drive. It took all her control not to mash the gas pedal, but she did not want to squeal the tires.

She could see lights coming on in various hotel rooms as she drove through the parking lot. She just hoped no one had seen her white Jeep.

She turned onto the road and fell in line with the traffic, making sure not to speed. She was shaking badly and sweat was pouring off her forehead. She thought her heart was going to explode out of her chest.

She continued driving until she was a few miles out of town. Her body was starting to fail her. Her head was pounding, and the rush of blood was causing her vision to blur. She could feel that she was starting to swerve on the road. She saw a department store parking lot and pulled in.

She was very dizzy now, but she needed to put the rifle away. She managed to get the rifle into the case and push the seat back down. She laid down and covered herself up with the blanket. She closed her eyes and expected to relive what she had just done.

But all she saw was blackness.

Sunday – Payton Becvar

Payton Becvar hung up the phone and slumped down in his desk chair. He was at his office in the police station surrounded by large stacks of case files. A million thoughts ran through his mind, but none of them made any sense. Nothing about what he had just heard made any sense.

Jack was dead and so was Tom. But how and why? It didn't make any sense. Could Jim have said something? No, that wasn't possible. Jim was loyal, and prison had never shaken him before. Was it one of their victims? No, that was not possible either. Their victims were all dead or accounted for, plus what young girl could take out two grown men living in different cities?

Maybe it was just a coincidence. But what were the chances of that? Both men being shot, murdered, by a rifle. There was no doubt it was a deliberate attack, and he had to assume that he was next. He had to get out of town. He needed to get to the cabin to see if he could make sense of things.

He went into the police captain's office and told him that he needed to take a couple days off to deal with a family emergency. Then he drove to his house, making sure to check every street corner along the way.

At his house he grabbed a large canvas duffel bag

and started filling it with supplies. He took his tactical shotgun, a forty-five caliber pistol, and his K-bar. He threw in a change of clothes and a few boxes of ammo. He tossed the bag into his truck and headed out of town.

He wanted to get to the cabin at Greers Ferry Lake by nightfall.

The Hard Way

The sun shining through the window woke Sarah. She had soaked through her sweatshirt, and her head still pounded. She grabbed a couple bottles of water from the back and downed one. She cracked the seal on the second bottle and used it to swallow a handful of pills.

She felt horrible, but she was at least functioning now. She crawled into the front seat and looked around the barren lot of the supermarket. It had been such a risk stopping at this place last night, but she didn't have any choice. It was unlikely that she could have made it much further.

She pulled out of the parking lot and back onto the highway. She stopped at a gas station to use the bathroom and splash some water on her face. Looking at herself in the mirror she looked sickly. Her skin was pale and her eyes were dark and sunken. She needed more sleep.

She finished the drive back to the resort, arriving before seven. She parked in the back of the hotel and used her key card to access the back entrance. As soon as she reached her room, she crawled into bed.

At a little after noon the maid woke her up, but Sarah shooed her away saying she did not need any service. She felt a little better now. At least she wasn't so tired, and her headache had subsided a bit. She ordered room service, another round of chicken and vegetables. Then she called Lucas to check in. He could tell that she was not feeling well, but she did her best to put his mind at ease by telling him she stayed up too late the night before.

After eating half her meal, she took a long shower. The hot water felt good against her skin. The last two days had been hard on her worn out old body, but she needed to push it even harder to finish her mission. The last leg of her journey was the riskiest and would require a little luck.

She had predicted that the news of Tom and Jackson's death would draw Payton to the cabin. He would undoubtedly want to stay away from home knowing that someone was likely after him, and the cabin was the logical safe place for him to run to.

Her tired body had compromised her timeline, and now she needed to hurry to get to the cabin before him. She had no idea how long it would take him to discover the news of the two murders. She just had to hope that she still had time to get to the cabin and get in place.

She finished getting dressed and packed up her suitcase. She didn't want any record of her checking out that afternoon, so she left out the back door of the hotel and stored her bags in the back of the Wrangler.

She then drove the hour and a half to Greers Ferry Lake. Once at the lake, she found a parking spot at the trail head and pulled out the map of the area she had printed. She looked around at the landmarks and was fairly certain she knew how to reach the cabin from her location. It would be about a two mile walk down the trail, then about a quarter mile through the woods.

She thought about taking the rifle with her but knew she did not have the strength to carry the twenty-five pound load that far. Instead, she would have to rely on her Glock pistol. She stuck the pistol and two full magazines into a drawstring backpack along with two bottles of water and a protein bar.

She slipped on the backpack and headed down the trail, looking at the map every few hundred feet to make sure she didn't miss her turnoff. Once she saw a sharp bend in the trail, she knew she had made it to the turnoff point. She was winded now and her side hurt. Too much energy had been expended over the past three days, and she was paying for it now.

She walked a little ways into the woods before finding a stump to rest on. It would have to be a short rest. She was still hopeful that she could beat Payton Becvar to the cabin. In her current condition, her only hope was to use the element of surprise to take down the seasoned detective.

The rest of the journey went much slower as she trudged through the dense woods. Every step caused her muscles to spasm. Her head had never stopped hurting, and the dull ache was getting worse every minute.

She was breathing heavily by the time she saw the cabin peek through the woods. She moved in closer and circled around so that she could see the front of the building. There were no cars parked in front and no lights could be seen through the front windows. She took her time circling around the house looking for any signs of life.

The place was empty, so she walked onto the porch and looked into the windows to confirm that no one was in the area. She tried the front door, but it was locked. She hadn't seen a back door, so she walked over to one of the windows and started pulling on it. It budged open just a bit, but it was enough for her to slip her hand under. She pulled up hard and it slid open about eighteen inches, just enough.

She leaned against the windowsill, nearly falling over from dizziness. Just the act of pulling up the window had sapped her energy. She understood she was now in a precarious situation. There was no way she was going to make it back to the car.

Maybe she could stumble into the woods and hide out there until she had time to rest. She wasn't even sure she could make it that far. Looking through the partially open window, she could see that the floor wasn't too far down. She leaned in and looked around the cabin. It was definitely empty, and it was filthy.

She held her hands out in front of her and leaned in further, allowing her weight to carry her forward.

She went tumbling into the room landing hard on her side. The pain of her bandaged chest made her cry out. She held her hands over her mouth as the sound echoed through the cabin. If anyone was in the building, they knew she was there now.

She pushed herself against the wall, then hunched forward. Her chest was hurting so bad that she could barely breathe. It took incredible effort to pull the drawstring backpack off and lay it at her side. Then she leaned back trying to breathe.

Looking around the small cabin, she could see that it was a simple open design. There was a table in the middle, a small kitchen to one side, and a couch on the far wall, along with a small stone fireplace. There was one bedroom in the back of the cabin and a bathroom off to the side.

The kitchen and open area were filthy. There were fast food bags, empty beer cans, and other trash and items strewn out across the floor. The debris was so thick that it was heaped up in piles in some areas. The table and counters were littered with dirty dishes, tools, and trash.

Sarah knew she had to get ready. The open window would alert Payton to her presence in the cabin, and she needed to get the pistol out of her backpack. But the pain in her chest was immense now, and her head was pounding so hard she could barely concentrate.

She tried to lean forward, hoping to get to her knees in an effort to close the window. Luckily, the surge worked, and she found herself kneeling in front of the window. She reached up and grabbed the top of the window frame and used her body weight to pull it down.

As the window slid to a close, she could not stop her momentum, and she went crashing to the floor. She rolled onto her back gasping for breath. A feeling of doom fell over her as her vision began to tunnel and narrow into blackness.

An Unexpected Visitor

Payton turned on the narrow dirt road leading to the cabin. It was dawn now, and the sun had dipped below the tree line. He slowed down as he made his way up the road looking into the woods on all sides for any signs of intruders.

He didn't really think that anyone would be at the cabin or even know about its existence. But he wasn't really sure what to expect. He had no idea how or why his friends had been murdered, but it was clear that someone had targeted them. He needed answers, but right now he needed to make sure he was safe.

He pulled up in front of the cabin and looked around. Not seeing anything, he stepped out of the vehicle and took out his shotgun. He pumped the action to chamber a round and slowly walked up the stairs to the porch.

He looked in the window on left and saw that it was clear inside. He moved over to the right window and peered inside. He saw a pair of blue jean covered legs and jumped back. He moved back in, slower this time. The legs weren't moving, but he couldn't see the rest of the person yet. He craned his neck to get a better view. He could only see the lower half of the body and part of the chest.

He could tell that it was a woman. He could also see a spot of blood on the woman's shirt. From her position, laid out flat and not moving, he wondered if she was dead. Maybe Tom or Jack had confronted the woman. But that didn't make any sense, why wouldn't they have called him.

He moved over to the door and slipped the key into the lock. He turned it slowly trying not to make any noise. Then he turned the handle and opened the door. He ducked low and pushed his way into the cabin sweeping his weapon right then left.

He closed the door behind him keeping the shotgun trained on the lady lying on the floor. He walked up closer, trying to figure out what had happened.

As he approached, he recognized her face. It was Sarah Fosterman. He scratched his head in confusion. How in the world had the old lady found this cabin? Could this frail old woman really be the one who shot his partners?

He grabbed a chair from the table and sat down facing Sarah. He was relieved to see that she was still breathing, which meant he was going to get the answers he needed. He pulled out his cell phone and started searching the internet. He had a lot to learn about this mysterious old woman.

Rude Awakening

Sarah woke up to water being splashed on her face. She coughed as the liquid entered her lungs, and she leaned to one side trying to catch her breath. Her side was still hurting, and her vision was blurry. A man's voice caught her attention and a wave of fear washed over her.

She looked up to see Payton Becvar sitting in a chair smiling down at her. He set the cup on the table next to a shotgun and picked up his cell phone. "Well, it's nice to see you are still alive, Missus Fosterman. You have been out for quite some time now, and I wasn't sure if you were going to make it or not."

Sarah was still coughing and trying to catch her breath. She propped herself up on her elbows and frantically looked around to her right.

"Looking for this?" Payton held up her backpack.

She lowered herself back to the floor knowing that there wasn't much hope.

Payton continuing scrolling through the pages on his phone. "You have been quite the busy lady, Missus Fosterman, or should I say Missus Blackstone-Fosterman. I would have never guessed that a sixty-five-year-old woman could take down Tom and Jack. And I have a feeling you probably had something to do with Jim being in prison as well."

He stood up, walked over to her side, and squatted down beside her. "I don't know how you found out about us or this cabin, but I assure you I am going to find out."

"You are a monster," Sarah's eyes narrowed as she spoke.

"You have no idea, Sarah. If you think what I do to little girls was bad, what do you think I am going to do to you."

He walked over to the table and sorted through the trash. Finding what he was looking for he held up a pair of needle-nose pliers. "So, I am guessing that you must have found out about the three of us from Jim. I get that, but I need to know how you found out about this cabin. There is no way Jim told you about the cabin."

Sarah needed to buy time. She needed to keep him talking until she could think of something. "It took me less than a day to figure it out. The internet is a wonderful thing."

He looked at her sideways trying to determine if she was telling the truth.

"You boys were quite the fishermen back in your college days. All it took was one picture in the newspaper to lead me straight to you."

He laughed loudly and sat down at the chair still eying her with disbelief. "I remember that picture now. We won the bass fishing tournament that weekend here at the lake. Let me see now, it was me, Tom, Jack, Jim… and Nolan. I almost forgot about poor old Nolan. He was a sad man, but he had such beautiful daughters. He didn't mind playing with other younglings, but he wasn't willing to share his daughters with us. We tried to convince him, but he was stubborn."

He stood up from the chair and walked around to Sarah's side. "That night he sent his daughters out into the woods and told them to call their mommy. He stayed behind to make sure we didn't follow, but Jack figured it out. So, we had to teach Nolan a lesson."

He stared out the window with a glazed look in his eyes. "I just wish we could have spent more time with those pretty little girls."

He looked down at Sarah and wrinkled up his nose. "I don't think you are telling me everything."

Sarah turned away as he brushed his hand on her cheek. "What more is there to tell? I found out who you were. Then I killed your friends."

"No, Jim couldn't have told you much. I saw that video of you visiting him at the prison. He barely said two sentences that day. Then you found a photo on a website. A nice lady like you would have needed more confirmation than that."

He stood up and walked around in circles trying to piece it all together. "Was it Janice? No Jim's ole' lady wouldn't know about the cabin. And she certainly wouldn't have talked anyway. She has too much to lose. Who does that leave…"

He paused for a second with his back turned to Sarah. She rolled onto her side, fighting through the pain. She pushed up so that she was now sitting on her elbow.

"Tammy. That's it. Tammy. You must have talked to Nolan's wife. She knew about this cabin. What a stupid woman. She must have known what I would do to her and her girls if I found out she talked. I will have to pay her a visit when I'm through with you."

Payton turned around just in time to see Sarah sitting up with her fist cocked back. She punched out hard with her left, slamming her fist into his groin. He doubled over in pain, crashing to the floor. Sarah launched herself forward, rushing for the table. She had to get to that shotgun.

She reached for the buttstock. Just as she touched it, a hand grabbed the back of her foot and jerked hard. She went crashing to the floor, as the shotgun was sent flying across the table. On the floor she quickly spun to her back and kicked the hand away.

She was dizzy from the fall, and it took her a moment to focus. As she lay on the filthy cabin floor, she could hear Payton standing up.

He was heading toward her. Slowly at first, but he was gaining speed. The punch to his groin had hurt him, but not enough to keep him down.

Her head was swimming and her vision was blurry. There was an ocean of adrenaline coursing through her body trying to help her deal with the pain, fear, and nausea.

She knew time was slipping away, she had to act fast. She began frantically feeling around the floor for something, anything that she could use as a shield or a weapon. The cluttered floor was filled with empty beer cans, boxes, trash bags, and other useless items.

As the man's shadow hovered over her, she clenched her eyes and tried to kick her legs out to move away from him. It was a feeble attempt that only served to scoot her back about a foot.

That small shuffle was enough to push her hand into something familiar. She felt a smooth round piece of wood and quickly wrapped her fingers around the wooden handle of a hammer. It wasn't heavy like the three-pound blacksmith's hammer that she had swung nearly every day for the past fifty years. This was a basic carpenter's hammer that weighed less than a pound.

Even in her weakened state, the full-size hammer felt like a child's toy to her. The unfocused adrenaline in her body quickly crystalized into one fluid motion as she slammed the hammer squarely into the man's temple, freezing him in place. He was hunched over, just a foot away from her. His eyes widened and his mouth hung open.

Sarah's muscle memory took over as she subconsciously followed through with her patented three hammer strikes. Like molding hot steel, the hammer made two more perfect strikes into the same location on the monster's temple. The final blow lodged the head of the hammer deep into the side of the man's skull and he slumped over sideways into the wall. He slowly slid down into a heap as blood began to pour out of his now gaping cranium.

She laid back, resting her head on the cold wooden floor. She could feel the sweat pouring from the sides of the tight bandages around her chest. She knew she was too weak to get up anytime soon. Wielding that hammer had taken every ounce of energy she had left, and now that the adrenaline was fading, she was also fading.

She tried raising her legs, thinking that might help her to roll over, but it was useless. The combination of pain and weariness were swirling together now. She closed her eyes for a minute in hopes that a little rest would allow her to regroup.

But closing her eyes didn't stop the swirling, and the blackness of sleep soon set in again.

The Aftermath

Sarah woke up to the sound of a soft banging, as the sun shown on her face. The light was blinding, and she had to turn onto her side to avoid it. As she turned, she came face to face with the dead-eyed detective who was still laying slumped against the wall next to her. She was startled by the sight of him.

She pulled herself to her knees and looked around the room, which looked different in the light of day. She knew it was covered in trash from the little she could see last night, but she didn't realize just how much filth covered the cabin. All the countertops and floors were covered in trash and dirty dishes. There were bugs and rat droppings on nearly every surface.

That's when she heard the soft banging start again. She wasn't sure if it was in her head, or if it was actually coming from somewhere in the cabin. She stood up and went to the sink. She turned on the rusty faucet and let the brown water run until it became clear, then she splashed her face and scrubbed her hands a bit.

She hesitated for a moment before cupping her hands and taking a couple drinks of water. The cool water made her cough, but it felt wonderful in her dry mouth and coated her cracked lips. She turned the faucet off and heard the banging again.

She felt compelled to investigate the noise, but not until she had looked around the area. She had to make sure that Payton was the only person in the cabin. She looked out the window and only saw the man's truck in the front yard. She walked over to the windows on the side and looked out but could only see thick woods.

She went into the small bathroom, but it was empty. She went into the bedroom and looked around seeing a king size bed, which looked out of place in the small room. There was a closet in the back, and she slid open the oversized door.

That is when she heard the banging again, but this time it was louder. She sat down on the bed and listened trying to figure out where the noise was coming from. She closed her eyes and listened. Then it sounded again, and she was certain it was coming from under her.

She looked around the room but couldn't find anything that looked out of place. Then she looked back in the closet and noticed a thick rug covering the floor. She grabbed a corner and pulled on it. The rug was heavy, but easily moved after she grabbed it with both hands. She pulled it out of the closet revealing a heavy door. She pulled on the latch, which allowed the door to swing open revealing a stairway leading to a basement.

From the outside of the cabin, you would have thought the building was constructed on a slab. The basement was obviously meant to be concealed. She looked down the stairs and considered leaving the cabin right away. Whatever was down there could wait for the authorities.

Then the banging sounded again. This time she was certain it was coming from below. She was even more hesitant to go down the stairs now that she could clearly see into the ominous and dimly lit bunker. A second sound caught her attention. It was the sound of moaning, and it was definitely female. She couldn't be certain, but she had a feeling it was the moaning of a young girl.

The thought of another defenseless girl being holed up in that basement spurred her into action. She walked briskly into the main cabin area and up to the dead body. She grabbed the handle of the hammer sticking out the side of Payton's head and yanked it free. Brains and blood splattered across the curtains as she shook off the larger bits.

She then returned to the bedroom and stood over the stairway. She slowly descended the steps. Once she had cleared about ten steps, she bent over and looked into the dimly lit room. From what she could see, the room looked mostly empty. There was a small table in the center of the room with an assortment of tools. A case of water bottles sat in the corner, and there was fridge against the wall.

At the back of the room there looked to be a cage made of chain link. She couldn't fully see into the dark cage, but she could spot the outline of a small human figure. She finished descending the stairs and looked around the small room, making sure no one else was in the area.

She looked at the table and winced at the collection of crude tools covering the wooden top. There were rusty knives, scissors, pieces of rope, and a pair of needle-nose plyers that were covered in blood.

She drew closer to the cage and could soon see that there was a small girl trapped in the cell. Her hands and feet were handcuffed together, and she had a gag of some sort strapped around her mouth. She also had blacked-out goggles covering her eyes.

Sarah's heart sank as she looked at the emaciated child, who had obviously been starved and brutalized. She was wearing a white wedding dress that was covered in dirt, blood, and yellow stains. She could only see part of her face, but she could see blue bruising on her cheeks. Her wrists and ankles were bloody and scratched from trying to pull out of her tight restraints.

Sarah found a set of keys hanging from a hook on the wall and started shifting through them trying to find the one that would unlock the pad lock on the cage door. The girl in the cage had stayed quiet until she heard the jingling of the keys, and the sudden sound caused her to start thrashing about and moaning wildly in fear.

Sarah knew she needed to do something to calm the girl's fears. "It's okay, honey. I'm not here to hurt you. I'm just trying to find the right key to unlock this door."

The young girl stopped thrashing and pulled her knees into her chest lying in the fetal position. She was sobbing. "I found the right key. Now I am going to come in there and unlock your feet."

She found a key that looked like it would fit handcuffs and reached out to touch the girl's ankles. The frightened child recoiled out of instinct but did not resist the second attempt. Now that Sarah was closer, she could see that the girl was very weak. The white dress had a large stain of blood showing in the center and the girl was holding her stomach.

Sarah unlocked the cuffs around both ankles, then worked to remove the goggles. "I am going to get this stuff off your eyes and mouth, okay?"

The little girl did not respond, but moaned as Sarah turned her slightly so that she could get to the goggles. She pulled the blackened glasses from her head, and the girl squinted as even the dim light in the room appeared to hurt her eyes. Seeing the woman seemed to calm the little girl for a moment.

Sarah unbuckled the straps on the elaborate gag that covered the girl's mouth. She slowly removed the thick piece of leather from her face and used the sleeve of her shirt to wipe the dirt, tears, and blood from the poor girl's face.

The girl tried to look up, but the pain in her stomach returned. She curled up holding her mid-section. With the gag removed, the girl cried out in pain. Sarah did not know what to do. She did not have the strength to carry the child out of the basement, but she also did not want to leave her there alone.

She needed to get a better look at the girl's injuries. She grabbed the key ring and found the key the cuffs around her small bloody wrists. She unlocked the handcuffs and gently moved her hands to the side. She saw that there was a two-inch hole in the dress in the center of the bloody area that looked like it could have been caused by a knife.

She worked her fingers into the hole in the thin silk fabric and tore it open with one hard motion. The girl cried out in pain. Sarah could now see that blood was pouring out of a hole in the center of the girl's gut. Sarah ran out of the cage and found a towel lying on the table. She returned and pushed it into the hole.

The girl screamed out in pain and clasped her hands around the towel. Sarah slipped her arms around the girl's head and did her best to comfort her. She knew the situation was dire. er only hope was to call the authorities. She needed to stabilize the girl to the point where she could go upstairs and get to a phone.

The child looked up at Sarah with watery blue eyes. "Thank you."

Sarah smiled at her. "It's going to be okay, honey. The bad men are gone. They are not going to hurt you anymore."

She could see that the girl was fading. The towel

had only slowed the flow of blood for a moment, but now it was pushing out from between the child's fingers. She tried not to cry, "What is your name, honey?"

"Maggie Powers." The blood drained from Sarah's face. She now realized the full repercussion of her actions. All this time she thought Janice Powers was trying to defend her husband. Instead, she was trying to protect her daughter.

She remembered the words Janice screamed at her as the police arrived at the Powers' house that night to arrest Jim. She said that with Jim gone, there was no one left to protect her family.

She had hoped the words were just the ranting of a battered wife, but now she understood. Jim must have been her only link to her daughter. She could no longer fight back the tears, as she looked around at the horrible cage. How long had this innocent girl been stuck in this terrible place.

At the end of the chain link cage, she saw a small folding pocket knife lying on the floor. The blade was covered in blood. She looked back at the girl whose eyes had narrowed into thin slits.

Sarah could not imagine the horrors the child had faced. Her Katie had faced those horrors as well. But this girl had obviously endured those horrors for weeks, possibly even months. Somehow, she must have gotten ahold of that knife and decided to free herself from the pain. If only Sarah could have gotten there sooner. If only she would have taken the time to listen to Janice. Maybe she could have saved this poor girl from some of that pain.

She looked down at the girl again and smiled, trying to be strong. The child looked peaceful now; the pain seemed to melt away from her face. "Tell my mommy I love her."

The words hit Sarah like a sledgehammer. "I will Maggie. I promise you I will tell her."

The girl closed her eyes and her arms dropped to her side. Sarah forced herself to watch as her small chest stopped moving up and down. She sat there with the child for several minutes before laying her down on the cold concrete floor.

Time to Go

The little girl had been dead now for nearly an hour. Sarah sat at a chair by the table trying to figure out what to do. She considered calling the authorities, but that would create questions she could not answer. She wasn't worried about her future. Worst case, she would serve out the rest of her very short life in prison.

She was concerned about her family. She didn't want them to know about any of this. It would crush her sons and devastate Lucas. She was also concerned about Janice. What would it do to her to find Maggie in this horrible place? To find out what she had done to herself to stop the pain.

She looked around the basement for options. Besides the table and cage, the room also contained a sink and small gas stove. She looked at the rusty gas pipes running up the wall. She walked over to one of the fittings and saw that a simple nut was all that held it in place.

She grabbed the pliers from the table and wrenched the bolt loose until she could smell gas. She finger-tightened the bolt back into place, then grabbed a rag off the table. She used the rag to wipe her fingerprints off the handcuffs and pad lock and put the keys back on the ring. She then wiped off the wrench and looked around the room to make sure she had cleaned her prints off everything she had touched.

She picked up the hammer, which she knew would never be able to be wiped clean and walked back over to the pipe. She loosened the nut again and wiped off her prints. Then she pulled the pipe down and could smell the strong scent of sulfur fill the room.

She walked to the stairs and took a last long look at pour Maggie lying on the floor covered in blood. She felt guilty for leaving the little child in such a horrible place. She walked up stairs and wiped down the water faucet. She looked at the area on the floor where she had fought with Payton. She was sure there were fingerprints in that area, but she would just have to trust that the fire would destroy that evidence.

She put her pistol and the blood covered hammer in her backpack and slung it over her shoulder. Then she lit a large citronella candle sitting on the table and walked out the door. She pulled the door shut and used the rag to clean the doorknob. The sun was warm on her face as she walked the mile and a half to her Wrangler. It was still parked at the trailhead, and she climbed in. She really needed to rest, but she knew she didn't have much time.

She pulled out of the parking lot and headed north back toward the Missouri boarder. As she got a couple miles away, she could hear a loud explosion behind her. She looked in the rearview mirror to see yellow and red flames shooting up into the sky.

She was still crying when she turned onto Highway 65 and turned north. All she could think about was poor Maggie and her poor little Katie.

Family Matters

The sun was already setting when Sarah reached the edge of town, and a light rain was falling. She had hoped to make it back home sooner, but the five-hour drive had taken its toll on her broken body. She had been forced to stop three times to take naps on the way. After each rest, she nearly gave up the thought of making it back that evening, but she had to get this over with as soon as possible.

There was little doubt that her back was covered in bruises from her fight, and the bandages around her chest needed to be changed. She would have to deal with those issues later.

She turned onto the gravel road leading toward the

Powers' farmhouse. She pulled up in front of the house and stepped out of the vehicle. Her legs were barely strong enough to hold her up, and she had to hold onto the fender to stay upright.

Janice Powers walked out of the house and stopped at the porch glaring at Sarah. "What are you doing here? What reason could you possibly have for ever coming back to this house?"

Sarah tried to speak, but she felt her knees start to buckle. She leaned harder on the fender, which was now supporting all her weight.

Janice looked at her, confused. She was still seething in anger, but she couldn't understand why the woman in front of her looked like she was on death's door.

"What is wrong with you? Why aren't you explaining yourself?"

"Maggie. Maggie says…"

The sound of her daughter's name sent Janice into motion. She went from rage to pure panic. She ran over to Sarah's side and arrived just in time to catch her as she started to fall. She helped her sit up with her back on the wheel. It was clear that Sarah was in very bad shape. And she was crying. But it didn't look like tears of pain. It was something different.

"Maggie says she loves you. I promised her I would tell you that."

Janice fell to her knees beside Sarah. She stared at her with watery eyes, not knowing what to say.

"I'm so sorry, Janice. I had no idea. But those evil men will never hurt her again. I just wished I could have got to them in time. Gotten to Maggie in time. I am so sorry."

Janice held her head in her hands as she sobbed. Sarah could do nothing but sit and join her in her grief. There was no comfort she could offer. The two women cried together for several minutes.

Once Janice had settled down, she looked at Sarah pleadingly. The woman wanted answers, not about the men, but about her daughter.

"She loved you till the end. Her last words were about her love for you. I don't have any more answers I can give. We were both just trying to protect our families, and we both lost our precious girls. All I can offer is that those monsters are gone now."

Janice moved over to sit next to Sarah. She was tired of being angry. Tired of being afraid. Tired of trying to be strong. She was ready to grieve now.

"The police will be here in a few days. I am sure they will have lots of questions. It's up to you whether or not to tell them that I was here or what I have said. I had hoped to protect my family from all of this, but I am at peace either way. I don't have much longer to live anyway, and I hear that they let you sleep in prison. I made a promise to Maggie, and that was more important than dying in my bed."

The two women sat for several minutes watching the sun set across the field. After the orange glow faded into the horizon Janice stood up.

"Come on, Sarah. Let's get you in the house and get you cleaned up. We can't have you going home in this condition."

Home Sweet Home

Lucas watched as Sarah pulled into the driveway at nine o'clock. She looked radiant in her blue sundress. It had always been his favorite. He got up out of his rocking chair and greeted her as she climbed out of the Jeep. He could tell that she was tired and probably hurting, but she was putting on a brave face just for him.

"You look lovely tonight, my dear. How was your trip?"

"It was productive, but exhausting." She gave him a kiss and pointed toward her small suitcase. He grabbed it and followed her to the porch. Instead of going inside, she stopped at the front porch swing and sat down. "Come and sit with me for a while."

Lucas sat down and held her hand. He knew his wife well enough to know that she was not in the mood to talk. He didn't have much to say himself. All he had done in her absence was work on furniture with their sons at the shop.

They sat for several minutes and Sarah leaned her head against Lucas' shoulder. "I really miss our little Katie." She didn't say it with sadness like she had in the past. This time it came out more as a statement. Like something she had just read out of the paper.

"Me too. But you will see her again. We both will."

Sarah smiled and stood up. "Take me to bed Lucas Fosterman. I am tired, and I don't want to sleep alone tonight."

He stood up and walked her into the bedroom. They were silent as they prepared for bed, and Lucas kissed her goodnight before tucking her into the covers. Then he crawled into bed next to her. He looked over to see her smiling.

He had been so nervous about her going on that trip by herself, given her condition. But the smile on her face was worth all the worry. No matter what happened next, he knew she was happy in that moment.

He turned off the lights and closed his eyes.

Sarah looked back at Lucas. She saw that he was smiling, and it made her feel warm inside. She knew the next few years were going to be hard for him. They had been together for most of their lives, and he was going to be a bit lost without her. She knew he was a strong man, and he would be fine. She just hoped that he would continue to find happiness, even through all the tragedy.

She closed her eyes and waited for sleep to come. She was so tired, but she was happy that the pain had subsided. Then an image appeared in her mind, it was Maggie. She was wearing a white dress, but it was not dirty or soaked in blood. It was clean and pretty, and she looked like an angel. She was pointing into the distance. She looked ahead and saw little Katie in her yellow dress dancing around in a field. She took Maggie's hand, and they ran to join her.

EPILOGUE

"The world is full of obvious things which nobody by any chance ever observes."

– Sir Arthur Conan Doyle

Odd Discoveries

Sarah's funeral had been a sad occasion like most funerals. Lucas had tried his best to keep it a small service that incorporated some joy and laughter, but those moments had to be forced. The pain was still too fresh from Katie's death, and the loss of Sarah came too soon for the boys and for himself.

It took two weeks for the dinners to stop arriving at his house. He didn't have the heart to tell the ladies at the church to stop sending them, even though he threw most of them away almost immediately.

He was still sad, but he was at least able to look people in the eyes again. He wasn't ready for visitors, but he felt like he should start doing something with some of Sarah's things.

He had no plans to get rid of anything yet, but he figured he would start by cleaning out her Jeep and working on storing away the tools she had in the shed. He parked the Jeep by the shed and started unloading the back seat. He found it odd that her rifle was tucked in the box under the seat. He thought she must have left it there from her last round of shooting, but that had been over a year ago.

He put away the rifle and shooting bag. He also found the rangefinder and a few random shell casings. These all seemed out of place to him, but he didn't put much thought into the random items. He moved on to the back, where he removed the blanket and pillow. All that was left now were some bottles of water, protein bars, a bag of gummy bears, and Sarah's draw string backpack.

He grabbed the backpack, which was heavy. He opened the top and looked in at the contents, which made him sit down. He could see his wife's pistol and a few other items, but what really drew his attention was the hammer. He removed the bloody hammer from the backpack and shook his head.

What in the world had Sarah gotten into during her trip to Arkansas? He sat down again trying to put all the pieces together. After a while, he gave up and threw the hammer in the trashcan. After forty years of marriage, his wife never ceased to amaze him. Why should that end now?

About the Author

Jason Mayer spent the first part of his adult life as a Marine Corps Combat Correspondent covering stories on five continents and more than 50 countries. After leaving the Marine Corps, he spent eight years working with government contractors supervising the development of more than 200 annual publishing projects.

Today, Jason is the partner in a construction company that designs, builds, and manages playgrounds and recreational construction projects.

Jason holds bachelor's degrees in Communications and Business Management as well as an MBA from the University of Maryland. He also has a PhD in Public Policy and Administration from the University of Maryland, Baltimore County. Jason lives in Columbia, Missouri with his wife, Angela, and two boys, Noah and Caleb.

Other Works Currently Available by Jason Mayer:
Parables of Lucas Fosterman
Barber, Chef, Ripper
Fuzzy Dragons & Wild Yetis: A Kid-Friendly Introduction to the Wonderful World of Poetry – Second Edition
Reported for Duty: Poems and Stories from the War Zone, Home Front, and Beyond

Made in the USA
Monee, IL
23 August 2021

75685410R00128